The Long Hungry Night

The Long Hungry Night

E. C. Foster and Slim Williams

Illustrated by Glo Coalson

Atheneum · 1973 · New York

For Gladys and Bob

Contents

THE PEOPLE OF THE STORY, IN THE ORDER
OF THEIR APPEARANCE:

NUKRUK AGOREK, *The-Friend-of-the-Singing-One.
An Eskimo boy.*

AREEGA ANGUN, *The-Wise-One. Nukruk Agorek's
father, and leader of the Eskimo tribe.*

OONATCHEK. *Areega Angun's brother.*

TAGRAK. *An Eskimo villager.*

TORIK. *Tagrak's son.*

LITTLE MOUSE. *Nukruk Agorek's brother.*

ANCIENT GRANDMOTHER. *Grandmother to Areega
Angun and Oonatchek. Great-grandmother to
Nukruk Agorek and Little Mouse and P'tik Tok.*

KORUMBLIAK, *Old Uncle. Grandfather to Keegor
and Ice-Lily and Summer-Snow-Shower.*

IMGOK. *One of the men of the village.*

P'TIK TOK (*Pitik Tok Sirenek*), *She-Who-Came-
with-the-Flowers. Daughter of Oonatchek and
Kiri. Nukruk Agorek's cousin.*

SUMMER-SNOW-SHOWER. *Old Uncle's granddaughter, and P'tik Tok's best friend.*

NATOOKA. *Mother of Nukruk Agorek and Little Mouse. Areega Angun's wife.*

KIRI. *P'tik Tok's mother. Oonatchek's wife.*

ICE-LILY. *Old Uncle's granddaughter.*

TULIAK. *Husband of Ice-Lily.*

KEEGOR. *Old Uncle's grandson. Brother of Ice-Lily and Summer-Snow-Shower.*

And the other men, women, and children who lived in the village.

Like the members of the wolf's family pack, most of the people were related to each other. Many of the men were cousins, second or third cousins. Some of the women had been brought from other tribal villages as brides. Ancient Grandmother herself had come to the village as a bride.

Sometimes a man from another tribe chose a bride from the village and took her home with him. And sometimes a man came, chose a bride, and elected to stay in his bride's village. Imgok had chosen his bride, and chosen to stay. So had Tuliak.

The Long Hungry Night

Nukruk Agorek's Harpoon

THE ESKIMO BOY crawled through the low passageway that led down out of the igloo and stood up. The wind off the sea stung his cheeks and nose. He crawled back inside and came out again, this time buttoning on a hood at the neck of his parka.

Inland, behind the village, the glow of the rising sun brightened the horizon far to the southeast. The first rays slanted across the still water in a tidal pool below the igloo. The boy noticed long crystal triangles frozen out from the edges. A dusting of snow had fallen, and the wind, sometime during the night, had swirled up the flakes and collected them in low places. Now, in the sunrise, he saw each drift of white sharply outlined in shadow black.

He could hear the dogs running through the dried sedge and grass. The familiar rustling sound had changed to a new hard rattle. A cold sound. From the hills, the musical calls of the wolves echoed in the clear crisp air. The-singing-ones, the Eskimos called them.

As he listened to the wolves sing, he smiled. They were his friends. One, especially. In the spring of the year, he had been caught out on an ice floe. A half-grown wolf had been caught there, too. As they drifted far from the home shore, the two had accepted each other's friendship and had shared hunger and danger. But there had been fun in the adventure, too.

Now, however, the wonderful summer was over, and they were safely home, the boy with his people, the wolf with his family pack. It had been the boy's tenth summer, the proper age, according to Eskimo custom, for a boy to receive a name. So now he was called Nukruk Agorek, The-Friend-of-the-Singing-One. The tribe, some thirty people, had so named him.

In their joy at his return, they had vowed never again to hunt the-singing-ones, but to share the hunting range with them peaceably. The wolves had never harmed the people.

Nukruk Agorek looked down to the sea, still free of ice. The men of the village were already launching umiaks and bidarkas and fanning out across the water. Until deep cold chilled the tumbling waves into rough ice many feet deep, the men would spend the short daylight hours in the boats, content when they were able to bring in enough food to keep everybody fed without using any of the stores of dried fish and caribou meat brought from the summer village. A seal would keep people and dogs free from hunger from one sleep to the next. A walrus would feed them all for as much as five or six sleeps. And there was always at least a small haul of little fish brought in by the umiaks.

The autumn was usually an unhurried, happy waiting time, the winter's hunting on the winter's ice still ahead.

Last winter had been a good season, the boy remembered. There had been enough to eat.

Across the bay, he saw seal and walrus moving about the far-out rocks. But just a few. Fins of fish and whale broke the surface of the icy water. But not so many as a year ago. And he saw a polar bear climb up onto a rocky island. But only one.

A year ago the tundra had been a busy place, full of all kinds of small creatures, ptarmigan and rabbit, and so many lemmings some of them had run down into the sea. Not so many now. But the sled dogs were full-furred and fat after the lazy generous summer, and the people, too, were comfortable.

At the shore, the boy's father, Areega Angun, and his uncle, Oonatchek, were bending over a bidarka, a two-man kayak, lifting it onto an inflated sealskin bag. From a nearby igloo, two men started down the slope of the small sand dune where the village stood. They waved to the boy, and he ran down with them.

"Few seal and walrus out on the islands," Tagrak, the older man, commented as they reached the shore. "And few spider crab on the ocean bed."

"True." Areega Angun nodded. "It is fortunate the salmon were plentiful in the summer river."

They looked out across the broad sea, between

the rocky irregular half-circle of the shallow bay and the long hazy curve of the distant horizon. Eight boats bobbed out near the offshore islands.

"There's a bear! A polar bear!" Little Mouse, Nukruk Agorek's younger brother, cried as he came running down to them, half a dozen sled dogs at his heels.

"Little Mouse has sharp eyes." Oonatchek smiled at the little boy. Nukruk Agorek didn't mention that he had seen the bear earlier, before he came down from the igloos.

"Are you and my uncle going out in the bidarka?" Nukruk Agorek asked his father wistfully. He fingered the walrus-ivory harpoon that hung at his waist with his jade ax. It was small and not very sharp. He had carried it all summer. Yet it was still fine for practicing, and he had started out from the igloo intending to go upshore, beyond the drying racks, to where several marked hides, hung over a thong stretched between two driftwood poles, served as targets.

"Perhaps the boy should go with you?" Oonatchek half-questioned Areega Angun.

"Well, for a little while, perhaps," the boys' father agreed.

"If you take an umiak, we can all go," Little Mouse urged.

"Or two bidarkas," Oonatchek suggested. "Nukruk Agorek can try throwing his harpoon, and I'll take Little Mouse with me so he can watch and so learn."

"You are kind." Areega Angun smiled. "Little Mouse, run back to the igloo and get camelinkas for yourself and your brother."

"And please, Little Mouse, bring the big new harpoon our father has carved for me," Nukruk Agorek called after him. Then he helped guide the first skin-covered bidarka down into the water. While he held the stern close to shore, the men lifted the second bidarka and rolled it down beside the first one.

Little Mouse came running back, and he and Nukruk Agorek each slipped into a camelinka. The coats of thin half-transparent membrane fit easily over their parkas.

Nukruk Agorek picked up a paddle, stepped into the forward opening, the harpooner's position, and knelt down in the willow-ribbed hull. Little Mouse climbed into the second bidarka and settled himself just as his brother had. The two men, who also wore camelinkas over their parkas, tied each boy's coat down around the raised rim of the opening in which he sat.

"Do we *have* to be tied in?" impatient Little Mouse asked.

"Storms come up quickly," his uncle told him. "Or something in the water—a small seal, a fish even—might capsize us. If you get wet, so will I, you know. And that water's cold." Then he got in behind the boy and tied his own camelinka to the rim around himself.

When all was watertight, Areega Angun said, "Let us go."

They dipped their paddles in the water, first to one side, then the other. The two bidarkas moved across the water side by side. Little Mouse watched his brother, trying to imitate his strokes. Sometimes he leaned over too far in his efforts to do it just right and almost tipped the bidarka, but Oonatchek quickly balanced the craft each time it happened.

"Let's go to the island where I saw the polar bear! Maybe we can catch it." Little Mouse, in his own mind, was already the hunter.

"Better leave the bear for hunters like Imgok, and for the season of thick ice," Areega Angun told him. "You learn to paddle the boat without tipping it over." The bidarkas moved lightly across the waves, quite far from shore.

"Look, Father," Nukruk Agorek said, leaning over the edge of the bidarka, "there are fish. Big ones."

"Let's see how good your aim is," Oonatchek encouraged him.

Nukruk Agorek fingered his new harpoon. It felt big compared to his old one. And the back-pointed barbs carved along the thin edges pricked his skin. But the bone triangle fitted well between his curled fingers, and the polished smoothness of the flat sides was pleasing to his touch.

"Fasten your harpoon to the thong behind you," his father instructed him. An air-filled seal-skin float was attached to the other end of the long coiled thong. He fastened the thong to the harpoon, then fitted his slim driftwood handle into the hole cut in the wide end of his harpoon. He was ready. He pulled himself up as tall as he could, kneeling at his place in the bidarka, and looked down into the water.

His father reviewed with him the proper way to hold and aim the sharp point of the harpoon, and how to use the motion of his body to achieve the greatest amount of force behind his thrust when he launched his weapon.

Areega Angun and Oonatchek maneuvered the bidarkas, and Little Mouse watched and listened and imitated his brother's gestures, though he had no harpoon to throw. Before long he was making critical comments.

"Aim carefully," Areega Angun cautioned Nu-

kruk Agorek. "Always pick your target, a specific spot, first, even when you practice." He pointed out to the side of the bidarka. "There are several tomcod. Not large, perhaps, but well worth the catching. Choose one and aim carefully."

The shot missed by very little, but all the fish scattered.

"No, no," Little Mouse scolded. "You didn't hit it." He appealed to his father in the other bidarka.

"Please, couldn't I try?" he begged. "Just once?"

"First you learn to handle a bidarka and a

kayak," his father told him again. "Then I'll carve a harpoon for you."

Nukruk Agorek was pulling in his harpoon, winding the thong line back in precise coils. Another fish, shadowy and indistinct in the dark water, swam within range. He pulled himself up, poised his harpoon high, and took careful aim. Oonatchek and Areega Angun held the bidarkas steady. Everybody was very quiet—until Little Mouse whispered excitedly at him.

"There, Nukruk Agorek! Throw it there!" He pointed some distance farther out from the bidarka.

Nukruk Agorek looked. Instantly, he darted his poised harpoon out where Little Mouse pointed. The coiled thong played out through his fingers, all the way to the float. The thong was jerked from his hands.

The men turned the bidarkas quickly. Even Little Mouse didn't say anything. An empty expanse of water surrounded them.

"What happened to the float?" Areega Angun asked.

"I don't see it anywhere." Nukruk Agorek frowned, trying to puzzle out what had happened. "There's my harpoon handle."

They paddled the bidarkas close, and Nukruk

Agorek retrieved the long slim stick.

"I think it must have been a great big fish." Little Mouse was round-eyed with excitement. "And it dived deep down, and your float is 'way under the water."

"The thong is long," his father told him. "I doubt the water between here and the islands is deep enough for such a mighty dive."

"Could something have made a hole in the sealskin, so the air escaped and the float sank?" Nukruk Agorek wondered.

"Possibly," his father conceded.

"More likely the harpoon snagged in the rocks on the bottom, and the line is tangled in drifting pieces of waterlogged wood. That could pull the float under," Oonatchek reasoned.

"No, no." Little Mouse shook his head so vigorously that the boat rocked. "I know I saw a fin where I pointed, and Nukruk Agorek's harpoon landed right on it."

"That's right. I saw the fin," Nukruk Agorek said. "I saw the fin before I threw the harpoon. Then I saw the tail." He was very unhappy. "Anyway, I guess I've lost my new harpoon. I'm very sorry, Father." They paddled around for some time, but there was no sign of the float.

"There, there! See? There are more of them!"

Little Mouse pointed out toward the sea. The sun sparkled on a hundred flashing fins.

"I see," Areega Angun nodded slowly.

"Beluga—whale," Oonatchek said.

"It's time we took you boys back," Areega Angun said then. "Oonatchek and I must join the men out in the boats."

As he spoke, a call came from the shore, and they saw that all the bidarkas and umiaks had gone in and were drawn up on the sand. The men were waving to them. The women, who had been gathering roots and berries and fungus bits, were returning from the tundra, and Ancient Grandmother and Old Uncle were coming slowly down from the igloos.

They paddled quickly back to shore. Little Mouse was so curious to see what was going on that he paddled much more smoothly than when he had been concentrating on it and trying too hard.

When they reached the land, the men on shore helped hold the bidarkas steady, and as the four stepped ashore, they saw that a whale had been beached. Its yellowish-white skin still showed mottled gray-brown areas, so Nukruk Agorek knew that it was not yet fully grown. But even so, it was twice, maybe almost three times as long as he himself was tall. A dozen floats showed how many men it had taken to best him.

Everybody was saying "Nukruk Agorek! Nukruk Agorek!"

And there was Tagrak standing beside the great whitish beast, holding Nukruk Agorek's harpoon!

The Uneasy Feast

THE FIRST THING Nukruk Agorek thought, as he looked at the great sea animal lying so still on the beach, was how beautiful it was. Its yellowish-white skin was still wet and shining. He thought how swift and strong and graceful it must have been, moving through the sea. He felt a quick stab of regret for having taken its life. He was sad before he was proud.

"It is yours, Nukruk Agorek," Tagrak said. "Imgok saw the float when the beluga surfaced out near the islands. Your harpoon was the first."

"I knew there was a fish where you threw your harpoon," Little Mouse said. "I saw it. But so big! I didn't know it was so big!"

"What has been brought in?" Ancient Grandmother asked as she and Old Uncle reached the beach. Then they saw the white whale.

"Oh," said Old Uncle in a strange voice. "Beluga."

Tagrak put the harpoon in Nukruk Agorek's hand. The boy looked up in gratitude. "I thought it was lost," he said. "And my father had just carved it for me."

"Now you have it back," Torik, son of Tagrak, said. "And with whale attached."

All the men and women were generous in their praise of Nukruk Agorek. But they did not seem as happy as they generally were when the hunters were successful. The hunt, by boat, from the ice, or on land, was hard work. It was no game. It was not fun. The men hunted because the village needed food. The spirit of the animal was always reverenced, and its forgiveness asked at the kill.

The whale would provide food for all the families and the sled dogs for many sleeps, and for that all seemed thankful. Yet Nukruk Agorek felt that the men and women were unusually sober. Even his father.

Some of the younger men were perhaps a little envious. Nukruk Agorek's honor, to throw the first harpoon, was a goal many of them twice his years had not yet achieved. But that did not explain everything. At the back of his mind, Nukruk Agorek felt uneasy, though he didn't know why.

"You must begin allotting the portions for the families," said Imgok, who had been the first to see the float rise through the water and had hurled the second harpoon.

"Will you help me, Imgok?" he asked. He knew that that was the courteous thing to do. Then he turned to Areega Angun. "And since my brother first saw the whale, although I threw the harpoon, the honor should be equally his, I think. Is that not right, my father?"

Areega Angun and the other men agreed that that was proper. So the two boys and Imgok conferred together. Then Nukruk Agorek and Little Mouse indicated a portion—a choice, generous portion—they wished to bestow on the hurler of the second harpoon. And they asked him to direct the rest of the apportioning for them, to which he graciously agreed.

One thing more Nukruk Agorek wanted. He consulted his father. This was the first harvest of his harpoon. While he and the wolf had wandered lost, Agorek, the wolf, had usually been the provider. Nukruk Agorek had brought nothing down with his harpoon. Fish he had caught in a basket he had woven of willow shoots. But the wolf had proved the more skillful hunter.

"Since there is plenty for everyone," he said, "could I ask Imgok to put aside a small portion for Agorek?"

"I think the request is justified." Areega Angun smiled. "What do you think, Imgok?"

"Sharing with a friend is wise as well as pleasant." Imgok nodded as he spoke.

Then everybody was busy. The men used every stick of driftwood that would serve, to set up more drying racks to preserve the meat. And the boys and girls were sent to collect small bits of driftwood and short willow twigs, and a little of the harsh dry grass that grew in clumps on the dunes along the shore.

With these bits, a small fire was set, and pieces of the fresh meat were suspended above it on long willow wands pushed down in the sand. Enough was roasted to satisfy everyone's hunger. Soon there was smiling and joking and talking everywhere. The children and the dogs ate until they were full and sleepy.

"Oh, I like it like this, when everybody's happy," P'tik Tok, Oonatchek's daughter, said to her cousins.

"Not everybody seemed glad when we brought the whale in," Little Mouse observed.

"I know. I noticed that," Nukruk Agorek said. "And I wonder why."

P'tik Tok and Little Mouse shook their heads. They didn't know either.

The short day was long past, but once they had eaten, the men and women worked on. There must be no waste. Every part of an animal was useful. Even the bones, frozen and brittle, could provide nourishment, at least for the dogs. And a day might come when they'd need it. The fat furnished oil for the lamps. And the great curved ribs made fine sharp knives.

"Well, we are full and content, for now," Old Uncle said, "whatever comes later." The other men nodded, but frowned and were silent.

"The weather is very good for drying the meat," Natooka said. "Freezing in the darkness and thawing by daylight, in six sleeps it will be dried and ready to store."

"Whatever comes later." Tagrak echoed Old Uncle's remark. Nukruk Agorek wondered what they meant. He wanted to ask but somehow couldn't. He went on filling sealskin bags with small pieces of the skin of the beluga, which by a sort of pickling or fermenting process became muktuk.

"I love muktuk," Little Mouse said. It was the favorite food of all the children. Natooka smiled at her younger son fondly, but even while she smiled there was a worried frown between her eyes. Nukruk Agorek noticed, and worried too.

The freezing chill of the long autumn night had already begun to stiffen the strips of whale meat crowding the drying racks by the time the weary workers retired to the igloos. Nukruk Agorek and Little Mouse were so sleepy they tumbled into their bed of fur pelts without a word.

In the morning, Nukruk Agorek was still think-of the same thing. But he didn't speak of it. The men were launching the boats, and he and Little Mouse ran down to the shore. Just maybe they'd have a chance to go along again. The men were intent on their work, anxious to be on their way out from shore. The boys helped however they could and didn't even hint, let alone ask, to go along.

At the village, Ancient Grandmother kept an eye on the few small children. P'tik Tok and Summer-Snow-Shower helped. The women were out on the tundra again, looking for whatever they might find of late ripening berries and roots, and the mushroomlike bits that still pushed through the half-frozen tundra turf overnight.

"Come on, let's help," Nukruk Agorek said. He had intended calling Agorek and sharing some whale meat with him. But he was so aware of the worry and uneasiness in the village, he felt he must stay, to be useful if he could.

"I don't know why everybody's working so hard," Little Mouse complained. "There's all that whale meat drying to eat during the winter."

"But not so many fish being caught," Nukruk Agorek answered. "And it takes a lot to feed all of us, and all the dogs."

"Maybe there'll be more fish offshore," Little Mouse said, "and plenty of seal and walrus to hunt when the sea freezes far out and the ice is thick. And anyhow, there's lots of dried salmon and caribou meat stored back at the summer village."

They helped Natooka and Kiri, P'tik Tok's mother, with the gathering. When the sealskin bags were filled, the boys carried them back close to the village. They cut out blocks of tundra turf while the women sewed the sealskin bags closed. Then each bag was laid flat on the solid permafrost, at the bottom of the hole from which the sod block had been lifted, and the cut-out block was fitted back in again over it. There the food would keep, safely frozen, until they had need of it.

It was very late when the men beached the boats. They brought in a few fair-sized fish, but that was all. Next morning, they were down at the shore at dawn. But the sea and the offshore islands were hidden behind banks of thick fog, dark gray except where the early sun touched their tops.

"We cannot hunt what we cannot see," Areega Angun said. "Possibly we might fish the inshore waters."

Even while he spoke, the fog rolled in along the shoreline. While they walked back to the village, the fog overtook them and blotted out the early sunshine. Atop the dune where the igloos stood, the mist was thinner, and the faint yellow glow of the sun shone through.

Sometimes there were days like this, when the men could neither hunt nor fish. Late in the autumn, fog sometimes covered the sea and the tundra. And sometimes in the winter, the whirling snow narrowed the whole world down to the cir-**cle** of the igloos.

The men settled themselves around the igloo entrances and talked and joked. The children and the dogs clustered around them and watched and listened, or played among themselves. The women, as long as there was light enough, worked at their sewing. Some of the men played with the children—games, like tossing them high on a big blanket of sewn-together walrus hides. Even the men enjoyed taking a turn on the blanket.

Later they told stories or acted them out—ad-**ven**tures, exciting or funny, maybe true, maybe **not**. Sometimes with a lesson good to keep in mind.

The boys usually loved days like this. But today it was different. All the people talked and acted as they always did. But, even when everybody was laughing, Nukruk Agorek could feel uneasiness underneath. P'tik Tok and Little Mouse could, too.

"Maybe," P'tik Tok suggested, "you ought to ask your father."

"I thought about that, at **first**," Little Mouse said.

"Yes, so did I," his brother agreed. "But—well —now I think he doesn't want to talk about it."

"That's what I think, too." Little Mouse nodded. "Could you ask your father, maybe?"

P'tik Tok shook her head. "I think he doesn't want to talk about it either."

Tagrak's wife finished mending a torn thong on a sealskin float and called to her son. Torik stood up and coiled the long thong in even circles.

"I'll take it down and leave it with the others," he said.

"Maybe I could ask *him*," Nukruk Agorek said. Little Mouse and P'tik Tok liked the idea.

"Try," they urged.

Nukruk Agorek followed Torik down through the fog toward the shore. Torik, after all, was not much older than Nukruk Agorek himself. Maybe four years. Six, perhaps? Anyway, not old, like Areega Angun and Oonatchek. But grown up, almost.

Torik had already reached the place, not far above high tide, where the boats and paddles and floats were kept, when Nukruk Agorek joined him.

"I thought I'd come along and see if the fog is lifting," he began.

"Not yet." Torik shook his head. "It'll take a

good drop in temperature, or some wind, to clear it off. Probably take one or two more sleeps."

"Usually foggy times are fun," Nukruk Agorek said as they started back up to the igloos. "All the people together, and they talk and laugh, and maybe play."

"Yes, it can be very pleasant." Torik smiled.

"But Torik——" Nukruk Agorek plunged into what was worrying him. "It isn't like that now. It's all different. Something's wrong. What is it? Do you know what's the matter?"

Torik regarded his young friend with wide surprised eyes.

"You really don't know?" he asked.

"No, Torik, I don't know. Should I know? Please tell me."

Torik shivered and frowned. "Beluga," he said and shook his head.

So Many Beluga

"TORIK THOUGHT I knew," Nukruk Agorek said slowly when he rejoined P'tik Tok and Little Mouse. "When I told him I really didn't, he just said 'beluga,' and kind of shivered."

"That's *all* he said?" P'tik Tok questioned.

"**That's what Old Uncle said when the whale**

was beached," Little Mouse remembered.

The three were more confused than before.

Three sleeps longer the fog hung over the land and hid the sea. During the few short hours of light, the sun, low in the sky, shone through the fog, red and round, small and dull, like the ash-covered embers of a fire dying in daylight. The women sewed as long as they could see, and the men repaired the hunting and fishing equipment and worked on the boats and sleds.

Old Uncle carved a figure from the thick end of a walrus tusk. He was Summer-Snow-Shower's grandfather and very old, though not nearly so old as Ancient Grandmother. His carvings delighted Little Mouse.

"Some day, Old Uncle," the boy said, "I hope I can carve such a beautiful animal! But what is it? It looks like a polar bear with long legs and long tusks curving up and a very long nose. Or is it a nose? I've never seen an animal like it."

"No more have I," Old Uncle told him, chipping and polishing the walrus ivory with his smooth, sharp-edged jade tool.

"Oh." Little Mouse thought about that. "Did you just make him up? Why did you put such a long nose on him?"

"I didn't make him up. He is real. Real as the

polar bear, or the-singing-ones, or the dogs." Old Uncle paused while he skillfully chipped away bits of ivory. "Long, long time ago he lived here. Called mastodon. Then the ice came—thick, deep. Covered the tundra and the sea, even the mountains. All winter, and all the summers, too. Never thawing for many seasons. The length of many, many men's lifetimes. Then, when at last the ice melted away, men came back. Some of the animals. But the mastodon never came again."

The boys were silent for a long minute, thinking about all that ice. Then Little Mouse had another question.

"How did you know how to carve him, if you've never seen him?"

"I listen to my Little Man. He tells me. Learn always to listen to your Little Man. Then you will

grow up wise, like your father and Ancient Grandmother."

"And like you, Old Uncle." Little Mouse smiled up at the old man.

"It takes many years to learn to live wisely," Old Uncle told him. "Learn to listen and remember."

Nukruk Agorek thought about that. Listen to his Little Man. That's what he'd have to do. Listen to the Spirit he had been taught was always with him, to guide and guard. He would have to listen carefully. He didn't know what he had done. He couldn't think what it could be. But he couldn't help feeling that somehow he was responsible for whatever it was that was making the people so serious and uneasy. Maybe, if he listened very hard, maybe his Little Man would help him.

"Of course he'll help me," he reassured himself. "I know that. But I'm not sure I know how to listen."

He'd have to know what the trouble was before his Little Man could help him. That was his first worry. What had he done? He'd have to speak to Torik again. He went along behind the half-circle of igloos until he came to Tagrak's, the seventh one, at the far end of the village. He heard P'tik Tok talking.

"Torik," she was saying, "don't you like muktuk?"

"Sure," he answered. "I like muktuk fine."

"You told Nukruk Agorek everybody was sorry he caught the beluga."

"Well, sort of," Torik admitted. "But not exactly."

While they were speaking, Old Uncle came across the small inner circle into which all the igloo entrance tunnels opened. The finished carving was in his hand.

"White whale in autumn," the old man told the girl, "not a good sign. Maybe hunger in winter."

Nukruk Agorek turned and ran.

Next morning, when first light came, about two hours before noon, he woke. And he knew what he must do. He must do what he knew he should have done in the first place: go to his father.

But, although it was still cloudy, the fog had lifted, and there was no chance. The men were hurrying into bidarkas, going far out toward the islands, still half-hidden in shreds of fog. Natooka and Kiri and a number of the other women settled themselves in two umiaks to fish along the inshore waters. Each woman carried a long pole of willow or driftwood, with a hook of bone or ivory on a walrus-sinew line. And another shorter stick to tap against the line, to keep the hook bobbing in the water.

P'tik Tok and Little Mouse climbed into one of the umiaks to help paddle. Nukruk Agorek could have gone, too, but nobody especially asked him. Not even his mother. Maybe they'd rather he didn't go with them. "Not a good sign," Old Uncle had said.

The boy helped launch the loaded umiaks and then turned back, worried and bewildered, the frolicking dogs at his heels. He dragged himself up the slope, comforted by the dogs' affectionate attention, but responding only halfheartedly to their coaxing invitations to play.

He found Ancient Grandmother in a sheltered corner beside the entrance to their igloo, and he threw himself down beside her. There, out of the way of the wind and the occasional flurries of wet snow, it was quite comfortable.

"How is it you're not out helping paddle the umiaks?" she asked. "I know you would rather be with your father, but, although your harpoon found the white whale, you have experienced too few winters to be trustworthy in the sea hunt."

The boy nodded, confessing his disappointment.

"You grew tall and strong this past summer

with the-singing-one," she went on. "The women in the umiaks could have used your help."

"I don't think they wanted me." Nukruk Agorek hung his head.

"Why is that? What could the reason be?"

"Oh, Ancient Grandmother, I don't know! I really don't know!" Confused and troubled, he looked up at his great-grandmother. "I knew that I had done wrong last spring when I was mean to Little Mouse and made P'tik Tok cry. But now I really don't know."

"Yet something disturbs you?" Ancient Grandmother questioned.

"Well, ever since my harpoon was first in the white whale, it has been different. Old Uncle and lots of others seem not glad about me at all."

"So you think nobody likes you. You are shamed."

"Yes, it must be so. But I don't know why! When I asked Torik, he just said 'beluga,' and sort of shivered. And that's all Old Uncle said when you and he came down to the beach to see what had been brought in. What did I do? Or do wrong?"

"It is as foolish to take offense where none is intended as to be guilty of giving offense," his great-grandmother warned.

"But Old Uncle said my catching the beluga was a bad sign," Nukruk Agorek insisted. "I heard him say so."

"Old Uncle worries like an old woman," Ancient Grandmother snapped. "Your catching the beluga took great skill. It is keeping us from hunger these many sleeps. There can be no blame attached to that."

"Then I didn't do anything wrong?" Could he believe it? For days he had felt as though he were living with a heavy rock on his heart. On his stomach, was how it felt. He took a deep, free breath.

"Of course not. To catch a beluga takes great skill or good fortune," Ancient Grandmother said. "And whether fish and sea beasts are plentiful, or we suffer a hungry winter, your catching the beluga will have had little to do with it."

He helped her to her feet, and they walked to the edge of the down slope.

"See there." Ancient Grandmother pointed out beyond the men in the bidarkas. The clouds had broken and rolled back a little. In the low rays of the sun, a hundred great white creatures leaped and played, appearing and disappearing between the deep blue-green waves. The men turned their boats and paddled quickly toward them.

"So many!" Nukruk Agorek said. He pointed

downshore. "And look! There are as many more!"

"White whale always travel in large schools—many, many together. They live on the small fish, which are the usual food of the seal and the walrus and the bear, and of the larger fish. So if fish are not plentiful—and they seem not to be this season—many schools of beluga may leave the sea almost empty of fish.

"Is that what Old Uncle meant?" the boy asked.

"That is why he considered the beluga a possible sign of a hungry winter ahead," she explained. "But there are always beluga about, near shore in summer, out in the open sea when the ice comes—good winter as well as bad.

"I have lived through more than a few lean winters when no schools of white whale were near. Sometimes the fish swarm in the water; sometimes they scatter, and the sea seems empty. Who can say why?"

"Would it be so bad," Nukruk Agorek asked slowly, half-thinking aloud, "would it be so bad, just hunting beluga for a season? We never have enough muktuk."

"No, never enough muktuk," Ancient Grandmother agreed. "But beluga are wily and wary. Very swift, very sensitive. They come, they feed on the small fish, and they are gone. Before the hunters can get close to them. Just the brush of a paddle against a bidarka, just the whisper of a sound, and faster than a man can blink his eye, they are gone."

While they watched, the bidarkas sped across the water. But the leaping white beluga had disappeared.

"See there." The keen-eyed old woman pointed upshore. Far out, far away from the men in the bidarkas, the two could glimpse the splash and sparkle on the water where the beluga played.

The sun dipped below the cloud bank on the horizon, and the brief hours of daylight faded into the long clouded darkness. The men in the bidarkas, disappointed, turned their boats toward shore. The women in the umiaks paddled home and drew in their lines.

"Go down and help them." Ancient Grandmother waved the boy off.

He worked with the men beaching the boats. The women prepared the small haul, mostly tomcod (the Eskimos called them apgak), and hung the sliced fish across the almost-empty drying racks. The dogs crowded hungrily at their feet.

"More dogs than fish." Tagrak's wife shook her head and sighed as she tossed the last of the discarded fish heads to them.

The people all talked and smiled as they helped each other, but now Nukruk Agorek could understand the unspoken worry under their pleasant words. For himself, he was so glad to know he hadn't been at fault, he could have laughed and danced. But underneath he was worried like the others.

Old Uncle might be right. Whether the beluga had anything to do with it or not, Ancient Grandmother had conceded the possibility that they might be facing a long hungry winter. Certainly fish were scarce and there were not many sea animals to be seen out on the rocks. Indeed, the people were already hungry, were already eating less than they wanted in order to save what they had. And the sunless winter night had not yet begun. He listened to the cry of the wolves, rising and falling out across the tundra. But they sang no song of the successful hunt. Agorek and his pack were hungry, too.

So Few Fish in the Sea

NUKRUK AGOREK watched the slow days darken toward winter. A shortening period of dim half-light, twilight, marked the middle of each day. When the sky above was clear, he could see the bright edge of the sun above the misty southern horizon.

Before the long night of winter had swallowed up the last fleeting midday glimpse of it, Areega Angun had sent four men with sleds and dog teams to bring food from the summer village.

"Bring back about half the cached food," he had instructed them. "We must hope that will suffice until the ice is firm and the good winter hunting fills our needs."

Strangely, when the long night of winter closed in, it was no longer dark. Except when storm clouds hid them, there were always the stars. So many stars. Bright as tiny flickering flames against the black sky, Nukruk Agorek thought. The snow at his feet reflected their glitter, and all the land was bright. Above him, the arcs and fans and waving streamers of the northern lights, the *akraliak*, ever-moving, ever-changing, lit the sky. Reds, yellows, greens—colors as vivid as fire one moment, pale and watery the next. And when the moon rose, the earth was light as day.

Only the still unfrozen sea was black. Darker than the sky beyond the stars. The men worked almost without pause at fishing from the bidarkas, coming in only when exhaustion forced them to rest, or high wind and wave and swirling snow drove them ashore. The women, too, spent long hours in the umiaks, luring small fish to their bobbing hooks.

They spoke together softly. "So few fish . . . So small . . . Almost none of the spiderlike crab creatures on the ocean bed . . . Other years, the sea bottom is half-covered with the very tiny ones on which the fingerlings feed."

All the children, except the littlest ones, helped paddle or hold the fish poles, learning to keep the hooks moving by tapping on the walrus-sinew lines. Some fish were always brought in, but for many sleeps there was never more than a little for everyone. Never enough to put any aside. Never enough to satisfy everybody. Never enough that the stores brought from the summer village

need not be used. Nukruk Agorek and Little
Mouse grew used to being always a little hungry.
The dogs foraged far out on the snowy tundra,
but they ran down no more than an occasional
white ptarmigan or lemming.

"The dogs are getting thin," Imgok said.

"And so are the women and the children,"
Oonatchek said, looking sadly at his wife and
daughter. Kiri's plump prettiness looked lost in
the parka that had been almost too tight last summer. P'tik Tok's red cheeks had lost their firm
roundness, now even curved in a little below her
high cheekbones.

"It is well the river was bountiful last summer," Tagrak said.

"Yes, that was fortunate." Areega Angun
agreed. "Even so, there is little of the stored food
we brought down left. Barely enough for our
present needs. We must hope the ice will soon
freeze thick and strong. And then maybe plenty
of seal and walrus and bear will fall to our harpoons."

"Yes, yes! Maybe," the others murmured,
wanting to believe it.

"But we see few sea animals out on the rocks."
Imgok frowned.

"And we find few fish bigger than the tomcod

in the sea," Tagrak added.

The hard work-filled time went by. Fewer and fewer fish were brought in, although the men in the boats ventured dangerously far from land, out into the stormy tumbling sea. The umiaks ranged farther and farther upshore and down.

"The fish have left these waters, that is certain," Imgok said. "And the whale and the seal and the walrus have followed. We have tried following the flight of the seagull, hoping the bird would lead us to the place. But we have not learned where the sea creatures have gone."

Nukruk Agorek knew the beluga had gone. He had watched. Only once since the day he and Ancient Grandmother had seen them had the flashing fins appeared in the harbor.

Still the solid ice did not form. Time and again they had wakened to find the sea water frozen quite far out from shore. But each time that the men had ventured out to test its strength, they had found it still too thin. It cracked dangerously under their weight, and once Torik had broken through into the icy water. Only the quick skilled help of Areega Angun and the others had saved him. As often as the sea froze, the force of the wind and waves shattered the sheeted ice.

There was less and less food. The dogs howled

their hunger, and Nukruk Agorek could hear
Agorek's pack echo the hungry cry out on the
tundra.

"Even when the winter ice is deep, the hunting
will be poor," Areega Angun said, troubled. "That
is now plain to see."

"Is it because of the beluga?" Little Mouse
asked.

"Ancient Grandmother said that is not so."
Nukruk Agorek still felt he had to defend himself.

"Who can say?" Tagrak shrugged. "They cannot have eaten all the fish in the sea."

"The seasons are never the same," Areega Angun told his sons. "Winters of plenty—last winter
was good—winters of want. The sea creatures
wander as the animals of the land wander. The
search for food is never-ending. You know the
caribou graze across the tundra, now here, now
there, wherever moss is most abundant. Then the-
singing-ones change their range to follow the caribou.

"We must find the seas where the fish and the
water animals have gone," Areega Angun concluded. "We have already hunted some distance
upshore and down. But we must search farther."

He sent three men and five dogs upshore with
a sled to see what they might find beyond the rock

ridge that curved out into the sea about half a sleep's journey north of the village.

"Go quickly," he instructed them, "as far as you can go in one sleep, or two. Not more than two. If—I shall say *when*—you find seal, or walrus, or bear, come back. Then we'll send out hunters with bidarkas. Umiaks, too. For where there are sea animals, there will be fish."

He chose Imgok to head a search downshore, and appointed three strong young hunters to go with him: Torik, Keegor, and Tuliak. How Nukruk Agorek wished he might have been chosen!

"A wide river empties into the sea a long two sleeps' journey downshore," Areega Angun told the men.

"I know the place," Imgok nodded.

"It may be that there at the river you will find fish and other sea creatures. Take an umiak and six dogs to tow it along the edge of the inshore ice."

The boys helped pack in rations for the men and the dogs.

"Only enough for two sleeps," Torik said. "Then we can supply ourselves."

"Take enough for five sleeps," Areega Angun directed.

"But there is not much left, and it is needed

here," Tuliak protested.

"And it may be we will find what we seek before we reach the bay where the river empties into the sea," Keegor suggested.

"Maybe, maybe." Areega Angun smiled and agreed. "But take rations for five sleeps. And when you find food, take only as much as you can bring in quickly, and hurry back. Then we will send more men with bidarkas and sleds to bring back more."

When they were ready to start off, Nukruk Agorek held the boat steady while Imgok stepped in. The pressure of the waves, cracking and crushing the thin ice, had made a ridge of broken ice bits along the frozen shore. A wide band of ice bits floated on the water, rising and falling with the crestless sea swells. The umiak moved gently with the movement of the water, and Nukruk Agorek listened to the soft swish of the ice touching against the skin boat.

Imgok rode alone. Little Mouse buttoned a long thong to the harness of each dog and handed the six thongs to him. The three going with him pressed long poles, willow or driftwood, against the side of the umiak to keep it just clear of the rough ice along the shore. Imgok gave the signal to start, the dogs barked and fanned out, and they all started off downshore at an easy trot.

Nukruk Agorek and Little Mouse—everybody else, too—watched until the umiak grew small against the dim twilight gray that showed above the southern horizon. It began to snow again, but not hard enough to keep the men and women from the endless fishing. The thin dogs went on foraging through the clumps of dry tundra grass that still showed, stiff and windblown, above the deepening carpet of snow.

Little Mouse shivered as the driving snow stung his face.

"Funny," he said, "when I'm hungry, I feel cold."

"And feeling cold makes you hungrier," Nukruk Agorek agreed.

After next sleep, Tagrak helped Areega Angun hand out food from the dwindling stores. A small portion of dried salmon for everybody. And a little for each dog.

"This is more than I need," Ancient Grandmother said and handed back half of what Areega Angun offered her. "I'll have it another time."

Old Uncle accepted his full portion. But Nukruk Agorek saw him give most of it to Ice-Lily, his older granddaughter. She held a baby, her year-old son, inside the warmth of her parka. She smiled at her grandfather, then looked quickly back downshore. Tuliak, her husband, and her brother Keegor had gone with Imgok.

"There will be plenty when the men come back," she said.

"Yes, yes," Old Uncle reassured her. "Then there will be plenty. Undoubtedly." But the worry in his eyes did not match his words.

The bitter wind and the snow added to the misery of the hungry men in the bidarkas and umiaks. Each day they brought in a smaller catch of little fish.

Every hungry villager watched upshore and down to catch the first glimpse of the returning men. The fifth sleep passed before bright moonlight revealed the men and dogs coming back from the curving shore above the village. They had pushed on through the storm to the very tip of the rocky point, but had seen no sign of better hunting or fishing.

The sixth sleep passed before the weary men stumbled back from downshore. The howling of the hungry dogs towing the empty umiak told the story.

"We found little at the river mouth." Imgok shook his head sadly.

"We went on through the storm, almost another sleep beyond the river," Keegor reported.

"But we found only small fish, like apgak, and even fewer than we catch right here," Tuliak concluded.

"The catch grows smaller here, too," Areega Angun told them. The exhausted men and the dogs were given food from the dried stores. They ate, then they slept.

Slowly the hungry days went by. Slowly the cold deepened. Slowly the ice under the snow built up, broke up, and built up again. But not far enough out from shore. Never thick enough to support the weight of the hunters safely. There were too many unexpected thin spots hidden under the tumbled snowy surface. Then the storm clouds blew in again, and the wind and snow drove the bidarkas in from the sea.

"There is no choice, now," Areega Angun said to the weary men as they rolled the bidarkas in over the uncertain ice. "We must journey to the river and bring back the rest of the food cached there."

"Yes," they reluctantly agreed, "there is no other choice."

"So early in the winter." Old Uncle shook his head. "But there is no other choice."

"We must wait until the storm passes; then we will go," Areega Angun told Tagrak as they struggled up the slope, heads down against the blinding biting snow. "Now we will rest. Then you and I and two, maybe three, others will choose the strongest dogs and go back to the summer village."

So everybody went into the igloos, hungry a little, and worried a lot. Nukruk Agorek wanted to help, to do something! He and Agorek had taken care of themselves all summer on their long journey home. But now he felt helpless. There was not much he could do.

So he worried and squirmed and turned over, trying to sleep, until Little Mouse beside him sleepily protested.

Outside the wind whistled, and the snow swirled. Two sleeps went by. No one could fish or hunt; no one ventured beyond the circle of igloos. The cold deepened, and the driven icy snow stung like sharp harpoon points. The dogs huddled in the long entrance tunnels and stayed there even when the men went out. The men went only as far as their dwindling stores, to bring back a little food for each igloo.

Tagrak's Story of the Five-Headed River Monster

A THIRD SLEEP passed. There was still no break in the storm. Nukruk Agorek and Little Mouse were very restless, confined within the narrow walls of the igloo. They were not the only restless ones. Soon, Torik and Keegor came in. They had been prowling from igloo to igloo, looking for something to do, something to help them forget how hungry they were. Imgok came to talk to Areega Angun, and Oonatchek came over from the next igloo. They lingered in the dim flickering light of the whale-oil lamp, the only source of light and heat.

The wick had burned down in the flat stone that served as a lamp. Natooka added a little oil from a sealskin bag to the bit remaining in the shallow hollow place in the middle of the stone. She rolled a new wick of caribou moss between her hands and laid one end in the oil. When the oil had seeped the length of the moss, she lit the new wick from the short, spluttering old one. For a moment the flame flared high, lighting the faces crowded around.

The men talked about the storm, remembered other storms. They spoke of hard winters, hungry times they had known. There were grim looks and deep frowns on faces that usually smiled easily. Then Ancient Grandmother spoke.

"Enough talk of storms," she said. "We have lived through them. We shall live through others. Now let us hear a story."

Before long almost everybody in the village had crowded in. Even the entry way was as full of people as it was of dogs. Each storyteller tried to outdo the one who had spoken before.

Finally Tagrak, a favorite teller of tales, said he had once known a man who told him of a very strange happening at the summer village of his tribe. Because of an injury, Tagrak's friend had been left at the village with the women and children while the other men went off to search for caribou.

"He said the fish that ran up the river stopped coming," Tagrak related. "For two or three days, not a fish. Everything was fine, sun good, water good and clear. But no fish. So he decided he'd better limp downriver to see why. A long way below the village, he came to a slow place in the river. Big willows grew there, some maybe high as his head.

"Seemed to be something very strange in the water. He heard a big splashing, but couldn't see very well through the willows. So he slipped up closer, very slowly, very quietly."

Everybody hung on his words. Even the dogs listened intently.

"There, right in the middle of the river," Tagrak continued, "my friend told me, there was a creature not like anything he'd ever seen before. A big, black shiny thing, bigger than a walrus. It had five heads. Four looked like seal heads, with long slim necks. And the four were reaching out on either side, catching fish. They'd eat one, then drop the next one into the wide, yawning red mouth in the big head in the middle. Not a fish got by.

"There were so many snapping mouths, so many flashing eyes, my friend was afraid. He crouched behind the willows and watched. How could he get rid of the thing? They had to have fish at the village. He tried to think what to do. Finally he crept up as close as he dared, picked up a rock, and threw it with all his strength." Tagrak bent down, straightened up, and made a mighty throwing gesture.

"The big mouth in the center stretched up, caught the rock, and tossed it back with so much force it was buried in the ground behind my friend. If it had hit him, it might have killed him! Then all the heads laughed. Or barked. It was a very loud noise, very terrifying."

Everybody was quiet, hardly breathing. P'tik Tok huddled closer to her father. Little Mouse shivered with delicious fright.

"My friend limped all the way back to the village to get his finest jade spear," Tagrak went on. "He limped downriver again—he was very tired by this time—and crept up as close as he could behind the willows. He waited until all four side heads were down in the water catching fish. Then he stepped out in front of the willows and hurled the heavy spear.

"But it was no use. The scaly back of the five-headed creature was as hard as shell. The spear glanced off as if he'd hit a rock. The four side heads reared up out of the water, each with a fish in its mouth, while the middle head grabbed the thong line and jerked it from his hand."

Summer-Snow-Shower giggled and hid her face in Old Uncle's parka. Tagrak warmed up to his story.

"So there he was, with his best spear gone. And then the creature lumbered out of the water after him. He was scared. He scrambled back behind the willows and fled toward the high rocks back from the river, limping on his bad leg, hopping on the good one. The thing didn't follow him farther than the willows. Pretty soon it slid back into the water."

Some of the women sighed with relief.

"My friend stayed in the rocks a long time, thinking hard. When he stopped panting, he crept back to the willows so he could keep his eye on the thing in the river. It was late, near midnight. As the sun dropped toward the horizon, the cold rose from the tundra. It made his bad leg ache. So he gathered some willow twigs and bits of dead wood from the evergreen scrub and struck a spark from two rocks to start a little fire.

"All the time the thing went on eating fish. Sometimes two heads grabbed at the same fish and fought each other for it. Very noisy. Lots of roaring and barking. My friend was so hungry and so cross, he felt like throwing another rock."

"I know the feeling," Imgok commented, and everybody agreed.

"But wait," Tagrak held up a finger and paused. "Just then, my friend had an idea. He tied short lengths of dry evergreen wood together with willow bark, two or three in a bundle. When he had ten, eleven, maybe twice as many bundles, he lit the ends. They blazed up, and when they were burning well, he threw them, one after the other, at the river monster. As each head stretched up and caught the flying fire, it screeched and plunged down into the water.

"But the creature still lay solidly in midstream. My friend had only one bundle of burning sticks left. In one last effort, he ran to the edge of the water and hurled the fiery bundle straight into the wide red jaws of the middle head. The thing choked, and smoke poured out!

"It rolled over, thrashed around in the water, all heads howling. It streaked downstream, with much splashing and roaring." Tagrak's words tumbled over each other.

"My friend said that scaly monster could swim faster than a bear can run! And he went as fast as he could in the opposite direction. When my friend limped into the village, the fish traps were already full. No more trouble with river monsters that summer."

Everybody laughed at Tagrak's good story, and they were all thankful that for a little while they had forgotten how hungry they were.

Journey to the Summer Village

THE NEXT MORNING the deep cold of the clear
Arctic winter stung Nukruk Agorek's nose as soon
as he scrambled down out of the igloo, with Little
Mouse behind him. Some of the dogs still huddled
in the long entry tunnel. But several men were
already out on the ice. Areega Angun, Tagrak,

and Imgok were returning to the shore.

The boys followed Old Uncle down to join them.

"The ice has thickened quite far out," Tagrak called to Old Uncle. "It will bear our weight safely."

"But there are few breathing holes," Imgok said, worried. "Let us call the dogs and get on with the hunting."

"Let us wait and consider first," Areega Angun said. "We found few holes where the seals come to breathe. I doubt the dogs will sniff out many more. We cannot, then, it is clear, expect to find many seals. I think we cannot delay bringing food from the summer village."

"If seals are few, it stands to reason neither bear nor walrus will be plentiful. Every man will be needed to track down those few remaining in these waters," Imgok protested.

"It is a dilemma." Areega Angun nodded. "Every man is needed here. But if, with all our men out on the ice, we still bring in too little, we will suffer hunger until food is brought from the summer village. Salmon and dried caribou cached by the river are far away, but they are there. They are sure. Food from the sea, this uncertain winter, may also be very far away. And certainly it is not sure."

"It is a journey of a long two sleeps," Old Uncle said. "I am old, and my strength will be of little help when you struggle to bring in the bear or the walrus. But I can drive the dog teams. I know well the safest winter route to the cache by the river. Give me two boys to scramble up on the high platform and hand down the skin-wrapped food bundles. In five or six sleeps we will be back with a comfortable hedge against hunger. If the sea hunt and the fishing from the ice go well, the food we bring can be cached here."

Nukruk Agorek held his breath to hear his father's answer.

Tagrak was silent. Imgok shook his head. Thoughtful frown lines deepened between Areega Angun's eyes before he spoke.

"You are brave, Old Uncle, and generous, to volunteer. But the trip is long and tiring for the strongest men. And in the hunt on the ice, your wisdom, which increases with your years, is more valuable to us than a young man's strength."

Still, they went on considering Old Uncle's offer. What to do?

"Perhaps you are right, Old Uncle," Areega Angun said at last. "You listen well to your Little Man."

"True, true," Tagrak and Imgok agreed. "Old Uncle listens well."

"But if you choose to go," Areega Angun went on, "it must not be with Torik and Keegor alone. They have grown tall and strong, but they are young and inexperienced. Imgok or Oonatchek must go with you."

Nukruk Agorek was so disappointed that he looked down hastily to hide the flooding tears he barely managed to wink back. He should have known Old Uncle and his father didn't mean him.

A shout from far out on the ice interrupted the talk. The six hurried out to find the other men lined up beside a long narrow crack, or lead, in the thick ice. All but Torik and Keegor, who were floundering in the icy water, clutching at rawhide thongs. A few men were stretched out on their stomachs at the edge of the crack, trying to pull the two onto the ice by the thongs.

Areega Angun called for more thongs, and Tagrak and Imgok threw loops, double for strength, over each man in the water.

"Slip the rawhide under your arms," Old Uncle directed.

Several men held onto the thongs. Others crouched at the edge of the ice, reaching out helping hands. Slowly and carefully the chilled hunters, weighted down by the cold water in their heavy pants and mukluks, were pulled up onto the ice to safety.

Helped by several other men, Tagrak and Old Uncle took Torik and Keegor, too stiff with cold to speak, back to the igloos. Then the hunters explained to Areega Angun how they had come upon the crack in the ice, leading in from the open sea toward the shore. In the water of the crack, almost miraculously, they had found a polar bear!

It had lolled sleepily, lulled by the gentle swell and ebb of the water. But like all wild creatures, it napped in snatches, waking warily every few minutes, ever alert to danger. The men had crept up slowly, keeping perfectly still, almost not breathing each time the bear roused. Torik and Keegor had gone back close to shore, where the crack was very narrow, jumped across, and approached on the opposite side.

At last the hunters had closed in on the great white animal, slipped a thong into the water under its hind quarters, and another under its shoulders. But the bear, suddenly wide awake, had thrashed around in the water and slipped out of the forward noose before the men could jerk back and hold it helpless.

It roared mightily, heaved itself forward out of the other loop, and slashed at the men before it disappeared toward the sea. Torik, on his knees at the edge of the ice, felt the sharp claws tear the skin across his right cheekbone. He had hurled himself backward and leaped to his feet, bumping into Keegor beside him. Keegor had lost his balance, grabbed at Torik to steady himself, and the two had tumbled into the water, right into the spot so recently left by the bear.

The tale was quickly told. Then the hunters followed the line of the crack seaward. The bear had probably gone far beyond their range, but they had to keep trying to find it. Losing that bear was a disaster. They would follow for a sleep or more, if there was any chance of catching it.

Areega Angun turned back toward shore with Little Mouse, Tagrak, and Old Uncle. And Nukruk Agorek, who looked longingly after the men; but he knew better than to tag after the hunters. Almost surely, later this winter he would go with his father. But he had to wait until his father chose to take him.

At the igloos, the women were busy attending to Torik and Keegor. Beside the deep cut across his cheek, Torik's arm had been badly slashed by the bear. And the ice, as they fell, had cut Keegor's leg to the bone.

"They must have food for strength," Ancient Grandmother insisted. She went with Areega Angun and Old Uncle and Tagrak to the carefully hoarded stores and took what she felt was needed. The three men sighed as she took a little dried salmon for Torik and a little for Keegor. There was so little left. And the long night of winter was not yet half spent.

"There is nothing else to do," Old Uncle said. "It will be many sleeps before those two are able to travel or help in the hunt again. You and Tagrak are needed out on the ice. The others have gone after the bear. Give me your two boys, Areega Angun, and we will bring back the food left from last summer's abundance."

Areega Angun and Tagrak looked at the old man in complete disbelief.

"Can you mean what you are saying?" Tagrak questioned.

"They are children, little children," Areega Angun protested.

"Nukruk Agorek can handle a dog team, can't he?" Old Uncle asked.

"Yes," Areega Angun reluctantly conceded. "Since his fifth winter he has been taught. He works well with the dogs."

"The boy has proven himself responsible. And Little Mouse is well trained for his years. Both are strong and healthy, and I think we can manage." Old Uncle put his arms across the boys' shoulders. "I think we must."

The boys themselves didn't say a word. Nukruk Agorek couldn't believe it. He was not a little frightened by the idea. Yet he wanted to go. And so it was decided. They worked silently and seriously, helping Areega Angun and Tagrak pack three sleds with the necessary rations for Old Uncle and themselves and the dog teams. Then they were off, those left in the village watching.

Out on the tundra, the wind and the deepening cold that followed the storm had smoothed and crusted the snow. The dogs harnessed to the lead sled trotted along steadily. The other two sleds hitched on behind added little weight. All the other dogs ran free, but they too held themselves to the easy pace set by Old Uncle. The boys, especially Little Mouse, were so excited they forgot they were hungry. Little Mouse chattered and laughed and capered around the sleds. Nukruk Agorek tried to walk sedately beside Old Uncle and act as though being sent on such a mission were a matter of course. But the stars glittered and the northern lights flared above him, and he was so proud and glad to be doing something useful, he couldn't help joining Little Mouse now and then.

The result was that Old Uncle and the dogs were still moving ahead steadily long after Little Mouse was straggling behind, and Nukruk Agorek was content to keep to the measured pace of the old man and the working dogs. The little company plodded on, the boys silent finally, weary and hungry. It already seemed like forever to them.

Finally, Old Uncle, tired too, said it was time to rest. They helped him cut blocks of the hard-packed snow, then set them up in a circular wall around him. Sometimes the blocks Little Mouse set up slipped and fell, but Old Uncle helped him fit each block into its measured space as the wall grew higher. Each row was set in a little more than the row below it, so that above Old Uncle's head the narrowing circle of the wall came almost together. Then Old Uncle crawled out through the side opening they had left. From the outside he dropped the final block into the top. Then they built a short length of low tunnel from the entrance. Old Uncle had chosen a place where the igloo stood higher than the outer end of the entry way, to keep out the wind.

Once they had spread fur pelts over the igloo floor, the old man, the boys, and the dogs ate their meager rations and settled down to sleep. Inside, out of the wind, all crowded in together, they were quite comfortable. Not as warm as in the sod-block igloos in the village, but comfortable. Before he fell asleep, Nukruk Agorek heard the hungry cry of the-singing-ones out across the tundra. Every time he heard that hungry cry, he remembered that he had never given that portion of whale meat to Agorek. Now he had none to give.

When they started out again, the snowy tundra glittered under the black sky. The moon shone down from directly overhead, and the midday glow on the southern horizon that marked the place of the sun was scarcely visible.

"We have a long way to go before another sleep," Old Uncle said. "The dogs are rested and they run faster than we can, so we will ride for a while. Harness five dogs each to two sleds, and let the others ride with us."

They rolled up the furs from the igloo floor, packed them in Nukruk Agorek's sled, and hitched the third sled on behind Old Uncle's. Little Mouse rode with Old Uncle. The teams set out with much impatient barking and excited wagging of tails.

Nukruk Agorek, alone in the second sled, gave himself up to the joy of skimming over the crusted snow, flying as fast as the eager dogs could run. The wind blew back the fur that edged his hood and whistled in his ears. As the moon descended, the northern lights, changing from purple-red into yellow, into green-blue, dimmed and flared across the sky, so clear, so strong, he could almost feel the rays beating against him.

"Look out for Nuumu," Old Uncle called. "She is tiring."

The warning jarred Nukruk Agorek back to attention. He hadn't been watching his team. Five thongs fanned out from the sled to the dogs. Four were pulled taut as each dog strained forward. But the line, second from the left, leading to Nuumu, hung a little slack. Nuumu was falling behind. Nukruk Agorek should have been watching. He picked up the slack rein and slowly pulled it in, so Nuumu fell farther and farther behind her teammates. He worked very carefully. He knew what to do. His father had taught him. But it wasn't easy. He hadn't had much experience. But he had practiced. The danger, the thing he feared, was that he might hurt Nuumu.

When he had pulled her back so she was running just in front of the sled, he braced himself and stretched out his right leg until the soft toe of his mukluk fitted gently between Nuumu's hind legs. Then with a quick kick up and a jerk back, all in one motion, he flipped her up in a somersault, and she landed in his lap.

So far, so good. Nuumu was a young dog, barely full grown. But the sudden impact of her weight was enough to topple Nukruk Agorek backward onto the floor of the speeding sled with his feet up in the air above the roll of furs. He could hear Little Mouse laughing, while Nuumu and the other dogs on the wide sled poked their cold noses into his hood and licked his face. After he managed to right himself, he unfastened the thong from Nuumu's harness and buttoned it onto Apga, one of the fresh dogs.

Now came the hard part. He set Apga in front of him, put his foot between the dog's hind legs, braced himself, and flipped the animal out in front of the sled. Apga landed running and was quickly straining at the rein, pulling his full share of the load with his teammates.

That first time was the hardest. After Nukruk Agorek had replaced Nuumu with Apga, he was able to kick out fresh dogs confidently. Always

very carefully, but without letting his fear of **missing** get in the way of his doing what he knew **how** to do.

He was so absorbed in his job of watching the dogs, he didn't get as tired as he had before. But he was glad when Old Uncle said it was time to stop. They had come a long way since last sleep.

Little Mouse Tries to Kick Out the Dogs

"WE MUST REACH the food cache by next sleep," Old Uncle told the boys when they set out again, walking behind the sleds. "But it is a long way to go."

Over his right shoulder Nukruk Agorek could see, far down on the horizon, the faint midday glow that was winter sunrise and sunset all in one. Above him, the moon, a little less than full, had begun its descent.

Mile after mile, the dogs strained at the leads. Twice Old Uncle replaced tired dogs with fresh ones. Behind them the moon dropped toward the horizon.

"Look," Nukruk Agorek pointed ahead, and Little Mouse saw, black against the snow, the sharp shadow of his short self stretching out tall as a giant.

The going got slower and slower, and for a while they rode. Even the fresh dogs tired quickly. They ran ankle deep through a covering of loose snow, spraying back crystal showers at each step. Weary Old Uncle slumped in the sled, and Little Mouse nodded beside him.

Nukruk Agorek was so sleepy his eyes felt scratchy. His head drooped, and he jerked himself awake.

"Hadn't we better stop, Old Uncle?" he called across to the other sled. "I know there is nothing to eat, but all the dogs are tired. Don't you think they need to rest?"

"Best we go on," Old Uncle said. He called the dogs to a stop and shook Little Mouse from his drowsing. "We walk now. Best we stay awake."

They plodded on through the powdery snow. One step, then one step more, the boys sometimes stumbling, sometimes almost falling asleep on their feet.

On and on. Silent. Nobody spoke. The dogs didn't bark.

Nukruk Agorek's cheeks burned, they were so cold. Little Mouse held his mittened hands over his nose, and his breathing grew icicles on the soft caribou hide.

"It's so cold," Nukruk Agorek said.

"Not shivery," his brother mumbled through his mittens. "Colder than shivery."

"Very cold," Old Uncle agreed. "And very dry. We are inland now, far from the sea."

They struggled on, even after they felt they couldn't go another step. The dogs bent their heads and dragged the sleds slowly. Sometimes Little Mouse fell a little behind. Sometimes there was a straggler or two among the extra dogs. But each time Old Uncle would call sharply. He insisted everybody keep together. And that included the dogs.

Two or three times, Little Mouse pleaded to stop and rest, just for a minute. But Old Uncle wouldn't hear of it. Once Nukruk Agorek stumbled and fell in the snow. He was instantly asleep. Old Uncle had to shake him roughly to wake him up.

"I told your father you could be trusted to help

me take food back to the village. Was I wrong?" The old man spoke sternly. "Sleep out here, and you don't wake up. You know that."

Nukruk Agorek was so ashamed he couldn't look at Old Uncle. Both boys were frightened. Their very fear helped keep them awake and moving.

At last, when they had long since stopped wondering how much farther they must go, when it took all their determination to keep on taking one step at a time, Old Uncle stopped.

"Look there," he said.

At last! Ahead, not far, was the gentle slope of a low hill. At its top, they could make out the bare willow frames of the summer igloos, dim against the dark sky. Below the slope, nearer than the deserted frames, was the cache, the high driftwood and willow platform holding the fur-wrapped bundles of food—nourishing dried salmon and caribou.

At the foot of the platform, the tired dogs sank down in the snow, snapping and growling irritably, but huddling close for warmth. The boys wanted desperately to drop down with them. But Old Uncle allowed them no pause.

"First we build our igloo," he insisted, "and feed the dogs."

The boys, more asleep than awake, stumbled after the old man. There was hard work still to do, and Old Uncle's stern rebuke had been reminder enough that out on the open tundra staying awake was the price for staying alive. Nukruk Agorek knew—his Little Man told him—that however sleepy and tired he and Little Mouse might be, the weariness of Old Uncle was deeper. The old man was near the end of his endurance.

What if something happened to Old Uncle? The thought shocked Nukruk Agorek wide awake. Little Mouse would be his responsibility. And the dogs. Old Uncle himself. The whole tribe, for that matter. There could be no rest for him until the cached food had been taken home. No rest until the food was back in the village far away on the shores of the sea. Nukruk Agorek worked while he thought.

"Come on, Little Mouse," he panted. "Help me get food down for the dogs." He was unloading a long notched pole from the sled.

"Just a little," Old Uncle said. "Perhaps they can do some hunting for themselves."

Little Mouse, a few hungry dogs around him, held the notched pole steady. Nukruk Agorek climbed up, worked one of the food bundles to the edge of the platform, and eased it down. While the boys worked, Old Uncle walked off a little way to where the snow looked rounded and pillowy. With the toe of his mukluk, he probed into the feathery light snow. It was little more than a generous hand's span deep, for it was not yet midwinter. The heavy snows would fall later.

As the snow fell away from the mound of caribou moss underneath, six or eight lemmings scurried out. Instantly some of the dogs, tired though they were, leaped after them. Others scratched down in the snow and scrambled after the small creatures they routed from under the moss.

The boys broke off a few of the cold curling stems of the lichen and shared them with Old Uncle.

"Fish is better," Little Mouse said, and dragged the sealskin food bag over to Old Uncle.

"We set up the igloo first," the old man said. "Neither man nor dog works well on a full stomach, and that goes for boys, too. Nibble a little more lichen while we set up the igloo. Then we'll eat."

The three cut snow blocks. Old Uncle worked slowly, cutting carefully, setting the blocks in a circle. Little Mouse tried and tried. He cut block after block, only to have each one crumble apart

when he tried to pick it up. Nukruk Agorek didn't
do much better. Only one block in three or four
held together.

"What's the matter with the snow?" Little
Mouse, tired, cold, and hungry, soon lost patience.

Inside his thick fur-lined mittens, his fingers were icy.

"What are we doing wrong, Old Uncle?" was Nukruk Agorek's question.

"Nothing. Little Mouse is right," Old Uncle told them. "It is not you, Nukruk Agorek. It is the snow. We are far from the sea. The air is much colder and drier here than at the shore. Less moisture to hold snowflakes together. Try over there where the snow has drifted."

He brushed back the loose top snow. Underneath it had crusted a little. Below the crust, they found that the snow had packed down a little. Blocks could be cut that held together well enough to be picked up and set in the igloo wall. But it took so long! The boys fought to keep going. Old Uncle tried to keep talking to help them stay awake, but at last the old man was almost too exhausted to speak at all. They worked on then in silence. Except for an occasional growl or whimper from the dogs, there was only the soft sound of their own movements, cutting and fitting the snow blocks.

Around them lay the cold empty tundra, limitless as far as they could see in the light of the glittering stars. The dogs foraged in the fluffy snow, but didn't venture far from the campsite.

Before the igloo was finished, they had all strag-
gled back and were huddled together near the
old man and the boys. Nukruk Agorek kept an
eye on them until he was sure none was missing.
Better hungry than lost and alone out there in
that vast white emptiness, he thought. The dogs,
he understood, felt the same.

Old Uncle opened the sealskin bag while the
boys spread the fur pelts over the snow in the
igloo. He fed a little dried fish to each still-hungry
dog.

"Best they're fed now, before they sleep.
They'll have loaded sleds to pull. And we'll have
to hurry. We must get food back to the village
as fast as we can."

By the time the work was done, the moon had
risen again and climbed about a quarter way up
from the horizon. It had been a long time since
the last sunrise glow had roused them. Before
they slept, the three ate strips of the frozen
salmon meat. It was so well dried it was not icy
at all, but tasted rich and flavorful. It hardly felt
cold in the mouth.

Again, as always, the boys awakened at sunrise, although sunrise was just a smudge of gray
on the dark horizon. The moon had climbed half-

way up the sky. Old Uncle was already up. Nukruk Agorek climbed up on the cache platform and eased down the food bundles to the old man and Little Mouse. Old Uncle packed the wide sleds, keeping the weight well balanced, heaviest in the middle, room for a rider and a few dogs in the front.

"That's almost all," Nukruk Agorek called down. "Shall we leave a few bags here?"

Old Uncle straightened up. He said nothing for a while. He's listening to his Little Man, Nukruk Agorek thought. Then Old Uncle sighed and shook his head.

"Best we take it all," the old man reluctantly directed. "We need it now. Food saved for spring is of little use to those who starve in winter."

Packing the sleds and getting under way took a long time. The waning moon was beginning to drop down the sky when they finally hitched up the teams and started home. The dogs barked and strained at the leads, as eager to leave and get back to the friendly security of the village as the boys themselves. Little Mouse trudged beside the second sled, but Old Uncle controlled the dogs.

They had been traveling a long time when Little Mouse noticed one of the dogs beginning to fall back. He told Old Uncle. The old man called a halt, and tired dogs on all three teams were replaced. A second, and a third time Old Uncle stopped and replaced the tired dogs. The next time he called a stop, he told the boys to release the teams.

"Best we stop here and rest," he told the boys. "The igloo we built two sleeps ago lies as far ahead as the summer village lies behind us. We cannot reach it before another sleep. Best we stop now."

Old Uncle began cutting snow blocks while the boys unbuttoned the lead from each dog's harness. Then they helped the old man. The dry cold snow glittered under the stars and the wavering northern lights. The moon had long since set. The snow blocks still crumbled easily, but not so badly as they had at the summer village. They worked on silently, too weary to speak. But they were fortunate, Nukruk Agorek thought. This sleep they weren't hungry.

Some of the dogs scratched in the snow, hopeful of finding a lemming or two. But most of them just slept. They weren't used to being fed oftener than every second sleep.

When the igloo was finished and pelts spread over the snow floor, Little Mouse tumbled into the furs, instantly asleep. But Nukruk Agorek followed Old Uncle out to the sleds, and together they dragged the precious bags of food into the igloo for safekeeping. Then the weary dogs crept in behind them, and everybody slept.

They had been away from home for four sleeps, and now, starting out again, Nukruk Ago- rek and Little Mouse fell naturally into the rou- tine of carrying the food bundles out of the igloo, gathering up the fur pelts, helping Old Uncle pack the sleds and hitch up the dogs.

"Before another sleep, we must go double the distance we have come from the summer village. Otherwise, we cannot reach home in two more sleeps," the old man told them. They set off briskly.

It was windy and getting cloudy, and an occa- sional flurry of snow blew against their faces. Old Uncle looked up at the sky and frowned. It was a worried frown. But the going wasn't really bad yet, and at the steady pace Old Uncle set they covered considerable distance. Mile after mile they trudged on. The very steadiness of it was tiresome to the boys.

The wind had grown stronger. They had been traveling a long, long time. So long, in fact, Lit- tle Mouse thought it must be nearly time to stop.

"How much farther, Old Uncle?" he asked.

"We have come about halfway," he was told.

"Only halfway?" Disappointed, Little Mouse was indignant.

"There's the igloo!" Nukruk Agorek pointed ahead.

"Yes. The igloo we built three sleeps ago, our second sleep away from home," Old Uncle said. "Let us rest a little out of the wind."

They didn't unhitch the dogs; just let them drop down and rest where they were. Then the three crowded into the igloo, and Old Uncle brought out a few small pieces of dried caribou meat he had packed away in the pocket of his parka.

It was a very little bit of food, and they rested a very short time. But it helped, and they started out again refreshed. Mile after mile they went on then, one step after another, the wind getting a little stronger, the clouds a little heavier, the snow flurries a little thicker and a little more frequent.

The boys had long since stopped wondering how much farther. All their attention was concentrated on just keeping going.

"It is far enough," Old Uncle finally said. "We will stop here and set up our igloo."

"We *must* be nearly home," Little Mouse said wistfully.

"It is nearly as far away as we have come since last sleep," Old Uncle said.

"Maybe tomorrow, if the wind dies down, we'll get there faster," Nukruk Agorek said, trying to encourage Little Mouse.

"If the wind dies down, we travel faster," Old Uncle agreed. "But we cannot count on that."

Heads lowered against the storm, they doggedly cut and set snow blocks, not hurrying, just keeping at it. And at last they crawled inside, thankful to escape the raw wind and the stinging snow.

They woke to screaming wind and driving snow.

"It will be slow going against the storm," Old Uncle said, "but we dare not wait it out. Already we have been on our way five sleeps. Unless the men have made a fortunate catch—and I think that is not likely—there can be little food left at the village."

Nukruk Agorek thought about his mother and Ancient Grandmother, hungry. And Old Uncle's granddaughter and her poor little baby. And the thin dogs, howling hungry.

They repacked the sleds, hitched up the dogs, and braced themselves against the biting wind. Hour after hour they struggled through the dark blowing whiteness. There was no sparkle to the snow. Above the blinding confusion of moving flakes, the heavy clouds blotted out the stars and the northern lights, even the moon. The three teams strained against the sled leads and kept close together behind Little Mouse and Old Uncle. Nukruk Agorek had been appointed to walk behind the sleds, to be sure all was well with cargo and dogs. So few they were, he thought. Such a small lonely company.

"Even the snow can't fool Old Uncle," he reassured himself. "He knows—his Little Man tells him just how to go."

One struggling step after another they fought the storm, heads down against the wind and the driving snow. Old Uncle hitched more dogs to each sled. They were all tired, but they struggled on bravely. Nukruk Agorek helped push when the way led over a rise, and helped balance the sleds across rough places.

Once the old man stopped the teams where a rocky outcropping rose above their heads and gave them a little shelter.

"That wind's so strong, it blows the air right

past my nose," Little Mouse panted, and took a deep breath.

"Some way ahead of us lies the igloo we built the first sleep out from home. If the storm were not holding us back, we'd have reached it long before this," Old Uncle told them. "I fear we cannot reach home before another sleep. We will stop at that igloo. But let us rest here a little longer before we go on." The old man was breathing heavily.

They huddled out of the wind a little longer, then fought the storm again. Nukruk Agorek noticed that Old Uncle stumbled more than once, and sometimes seemed to stagger. He worried and wished the old man would ride. Little Mouse had dropped back and was getting some help for himself by hanging onto one of the sleds.

There was no letup in the storm. And no end to their journey, it seemed. Every step was a battle against a wind that pushed them backward with as much force as they fought to move forward. It blew into their faces and almost smothered them.

Progress was very slow. Frequently they made no headway at all, but could only stand up to the wind by clinging to the sleds and to each other. The dogs crouched low and moved close to the snow to cut the wind's force against them.

Finally Nukruk Agorek wondered if perhaps it wouldn't be better to stop and try to set up an igloo. But Old Uncle shook his head.

"Not much farther now," he gasped.

So they went on, and at last reached their goal. When they crept into the welcome shelter of the igloo, although nobody said anything, they all knew neither they nor the dogs could have gone on much farther. They had not really come far, but it had taken longer than the greatest distance they had covered between any two sleeps.

The snow still fell when they were ready to start out again, but the wind blew a little less fiercely.

"I think it best we start out riding," Old Uncle said. "We must reach the village quickly. We are already one sleep late, and the storm may grow worse again before it clears. Even with the sleds loaded, the dogs can carry us faster than we can walk, at least part way. We will stop and change them often."

Old Uncle drove the first sled, Little Mouse the second, and Nukruk Agorek drove the third. "Call out if you see any dog tiring," Old Uncle told the boys. "Watch them carefully, Little Mouse." In spite of driving snow and heavy loads, the dogs, knowing they were on the homestretch, hunched their shoulders against the burden and pulled eagerly.

Three times Old Uncle halted the teams and put in fresh dogs. They ran well for a long time. Then Little Mouse noticed one of his dogs beginning to fall behind. Krik, he remembered, had run a little lame two sleeps before.

He started to call out to Old Uncle to stop and replace the tired one. But that would mean losing time they couldn't spare. He knew how to kick out the dogs. That is, he had been told how. He had watched his father. And he had watched while Nukruk Agorek and the older boys in the village had been taught. And he had been watching Old Uncle and Nukruk Agorek whenever they had kicked out the dogs. He had watched carefully.

He pulled the tiring dog back slowly. When it was running just in front of the sled, he slipped the toe of his mukluk between the dog's hind legs, and with a quick jerk on the harness lead and a mighty kick up, tried to somersault Krik backwards into his lap. But Krik was too heavy. The dog fell sidewise and was caught under the runners of the loaded sled.

Krik gave a high screaming cry. All the dogs

slowed. Little Mouse tried to drag the injured dog up into the sled, but instead Krik squirmed himself free. Dragging his torn harness, the frightened dog ran past Old Uncle and streaked ahead into the storm. He left a queer uneven track, and drops of red freezing into the snow. Little Mouse jumped from the sled and ran after him.

"Krik! Krik!" he called. "I didn't mean to hurt you!"

"Come back!" Nukruk Agorek shouted, running after Little Mouse. He stopped almost at once. He couldn't leave Old Uncle and the food-filled sleds. But he couldn't let Little Mouse run off alone. Already the snow hid the dog and the boy.

"The dog will head for home," Old Uncle said. "He will lead Little Mouse to the village. It is not much farther. Come, help me with the sleds. We may soon catch up with Little Mouse and Krik. Or else they will be at the village before us."

Agorek Helps

THEY URGED the dogs along, each minute hoping that the next minute they'd see Little Mouse and Krik ahead, beyond the receding curtain of the snow.

"It is not far," Old Uncle had said.

Nukruk Agorek raised his head and breathed

deeply. The smell of the sea! Yes! Almost home. Little Mouse and Krik had made it all the way. Nevertheless, he'd feel better when he could actually see them.

"Faster, faster!" he called to the dogs. "We're almost home."

Then they left the tundra and were running down the beach slope. Dim in the blowing snow, they could see the domed igloos. The barking dogs brought the women out to welcome them, Keegor limping along. All the other men, of course, were out on the ice.

Old Uncle sat slumped in the sled, too exhausted to move. The women clustered around him. Keegor helped Nukruk Agorek unhitch the dogs.

"What happened to Krik?" Keegor asked as they began lifting the food bags from the sleds.

"Didn't Little Mouse tell you?" Nukruk Agorek was so startled, he dropped the bag he was lifting. "He's here, isn't he?"

Keegor shook his head.

"Krik came home alone. One leg's all bloody. Limping, like me. P'tik Tok took him to Ancient Grandmother and Natooka. They're in the igloo fixing him up."

"Old Uncle! Old Uncle!" Nukruk Agorek raced

to the old man. "Little Mouse hasn't come back! Only Krik."

Once more the tired old man fought back his exhaustion.

"Keegor, hitch up fresh dogs," he directed. "You and I cannot go so well afoot. Nukruk Agorek, get your father—all the men. Tell them Keegor and I have started back along the way we came. They had better fan out to each side."

Areega Angun quickly organized the search. All the men, and most of the women, hurried out on the tundra, the same worry in each one's heart. How long could Little Mouse stay alive, out there on the dark open tundra in the bitter winter weather?

The snow had stopped falling, and there was less blowing, so the searchers were able to see farther across the level tundra. But they could see no Little Mouse. They called, but there was no answer. The search grew more urgent. They looked hurriedly, but very thoroughly, over every small rise of ground, investigated every lumpy irregularity that might be only an outcropping of rock. Or might, perhaps, hide a small boy who had stumbled and fallen in the snow.

"How far had you come?" Natooka wanted to know. "How far were you from the village?"

"Almost within smell of the sea," Nukruk Agorek told her.

"No farther than here," Old Uncle said. He had halted the team, and the searchers were coming together around the sled.

"Let us fan out farther," Areega Angun spoke. "The boy *must* be somewhere between here and the shore."

"We must find him soon," Natooka pleaded.

"We will find him, Natooka," Areega Angun touched her shoulder gently. "Be sure to stay close to Nukruk Agorek."

They started back toward the village, fanning farther out to each side beyond the trails they had made. They spoke very little. They were all thinking how every direction looks the same in swirling snow, even to grown men.

Nukruk Agorek knew that, too. Which way had Little Mouse gone? Krik had known just where he was going. The snow had not weakened his instinct. But Little Mouse? He went by what he could see. And he had not lived long enough to know the tundra very well. Where had he wandered? How close to home had he come before he lost his way?

Natooka and Nukruk Agorek stopped. They had circled out behind the other searchers. Above them the clouds had broken, and under the low half-moon the snow looked pale yellow.

Far away, inland across the tundra, a wolf sang. In the back of his mind, Nukruk Agorek thought of his friend and hoped the pack had made a good catch. When hunger stalked the Eskimos, hunger usually stalked the wolf pack, too.

Again the song rang out. "That sounds like Agorek." His own whispered words barely touched Nukruk Agorek's mind. He went on searching. Fear for Little Mouse drove him on, and drove all other thoughts away.

"Wolves," Natooka said when the rising trickle of notes sounded again. "Is it Agorek? I know the-singing-ones will not hurt Little Mouse, but. . . ." She could not hide the fear in her heart.

Areega Angun approached, and Old Uncle drove up in the sled.

"Is it Agorek who sings?" Areega Angun asked.

"I think so." Nukruk Agorek listened for the repeated notes.

"He might be calling you," Old Uncle suggested.

"Yes, he might be, but I don't think so."

"Perhaps you should go to him," his father said.

"How can I go to him now?" Nukruk Agorek

protested. "We have to look for Little Mouse! And Agorek is 'way back there." He pointed across the tundra. " 'Way back there toward the igloo where we stayed last sleep."

"Better go see," Areega Angun insisted.

Old Uncle took him part of the way in the sled. When the old man halted the dogs, the boy called out to Agorek, and went on alone on foot when the wolf answered. He had forgotten how tired he was. He went on a long way. Once he looked back to where Old Uncle and the dogs waited. Farther back he could see the searchers still combing the tundra behind him. The moon was dim on the horizon, but the stars and the northern lights now shone on the tundra. The storm, at least, was over.

Down a shallow little gulley that hid a stream in the spring, he came upon his friend. Agorek crouched over the still figure of Little Mouse. The boy's eyes were closed. The wolf was licking the pale face.

"Oh, Agorek! You've found him." Nukruk Agorek spoke softly. "How good a friend you are!" He knelt down and rubbed his brother's hands and feet, trying to warm them.

Then he called out, his voice echoing across the tundra. Before Natooka, in the sled with Old

Uncle, and Areega Angun reached them, the wolf gave his friend's cheek an affectionate lick, nudged his shoulder, and loped off. The-singing-one was thin. Nukruk Agorek could see the lines of his ribs.

In the sled, Natooka cradled Little Mouse in her arms. Areega Angun urged the dogs ahead. Nukruk Agorek and the others ran along. Little Mouse still had not opened his eyes when they got back to the village.

In the igloo, Ancient Grandmother slipped off his mittens and mukluks.

"So cold," Natooka moaned.

"Agorek was crouched right over him." Nukruk Agorek tried to reassure his mother. "I know he was trying to keep him warm."

Areega Angun said nothing, but with his eyes he questioned Ancient Grandmother. She sighed and shrugged.

"Who can tell?" she said. "We shall see. Wrap him in warm furs. And we must have a fire."

Nukruk Agorek followed her out of the igloo. Precious bits of driftwood were collected to burn. No wood was ever wasted. The smallest scraps were hoarded for the flames. There had been no warmth of fire in the village since Nukruk Agorek's harpoon had brought down the white whale.

Ancient Grandmother brought out two bowls made of dried clay. She sent Torik and Keegor to search under the snow for small stones. Smooth ones if possible. Less likely to crack in the heat.

"About the size of small duck eggs," she specified.

While the men were distributing portions of the food brought back by Old Uncle and the boys, and then storing the rest, she directed Kiri and Oonatchek to pick out several pieces of good fat salmon.

Tagrak tended the small fire, and when the boys brought back stones, she selected five or six and dropped them into it. She scooped snow into the larger bowl and set both bowls close to the fire. Breaking the rich dried-salmon slices into pieces, she added the bits to the melting snow in the larger bowl.

She took two lengths of willow wand of last summer's cutting and stirred the salmon bits in the water. Then, using the wands deftly, in the manner of chopsticks, she lifted one of the heated stones out of the fire and dropped it into the bowl, where it spluttered and hissed in the cold water. She stirred and poked at the salmon, and when the stone had cooled a little—warming the broth as it cooled—she picked it out, put it back in the fire, and dropped another hot one into the broth. She replaced a cooling stone several times, stirring and breaking up the warming salmon with the willow wands.

It smelled so good, the dogs, who had already finished the fish given them, came sniffing round. The people, too. But everyone was so worried about Little Mouse, nobody could really enjoy the food they needed so badly.

At last, when the broth was rich and steaming, she poured some into the smaller bowl and took it into the igloo. Nukruk Agorek and a few others followed her.

There was no sound in the igloo except the heavy breathing of Old Uncle, who watched and waited. Little Mouse had not moved or opened his eyes. Ancient Grandmother knelt beside him, and with a spoon carved from a hollow curve of walrus ivory, touched his cold lips with a drop of the warm broth.

At first there was no response, and Nukruk Agorek held his breath in an agony of fear and grief. It was hopeless, he thought. But at last the cold lips parted just enough to let the taste of the warm drops reach the tip of the tongue. Ancient Grandmother spooned out a few more drops of the steaming broth. Little Mouse swallowed, then

moaned softly and began to cry.

"Krik!" he whispered weakly. "Krik! Come back! I didn't mean to hurt you!" And all at once his eyes flew open. He was wide-awake and struggling to get out of the furs.

Natooka and Areega Angun tried to quiet him, but he continued to struggle until Nukruk Agorek brought the limping Krik in from the entrance tunnel. It was a joyous reunion.

Then Little Mouse was more than ready to drink up every drop of the broth Ancient Grandmother slowly fed him. Before he had finished it, though, he said his fingers and toes hurt.

"They prickle," he complained.

"Good, good." Areega Angun smiled.

"That's fine," Ancient Grandmother said. Little Mouse was indignant.

"That means they will soon be all right," Natooka told him. "It is a sign they are getting warm again."

"Now you, old man." Ancient Grandmother turned to Old Uncle. "Get back to your igloo. Keegor will go with you and see that you rest. And I will bring broth. I think you need it almost more than the boy did."

Ancient Grandmother
Addresses the Council

BY USING the food very sparingly, the caribou meat and salmon Old Uncle and the boys had brought from the summer village kept starvation away for many sleeps. Almost a full moon cycle. But the time came when there was little left. And no more to go after.

The men hunted on sea and on land. Nukruk Agorek took his turn with the men watching at the seals' breathing holes, and in the small dark igloos built on the ice. While Old Uncle and the boys had traveled to the summer village, the men had hacked out fishing holes and built the igloos over them. Nukruk Agorek remembered helping the year before. Using a sharp-edged wedge of jade lashed to the end of a long wooden handle, the men had cut through the ice. He remembered how the water, released from the pressure of the ice's weight, had boiled up through the hole like a fountain.

But last year there had been fish aplenty. Now it was different. The moonlight, even the starlight, flooding under the ice, made the water glow, and it was easy for the watchers in the small dark igloo to see any fish or seal who swam below their feet. But this year there were almost no seals, and the fish were small and few.

Time goes by very slowly when you're hungry. Especially when all you can do about it is sit in the dark and watch. But that's how it is with ice fishing. You just sit and wait, and keep very quiet. Except when there is a fish to catch.

Nukruk Agorek tried very hard to keep his attention on the empty glow below the ice, but he

couldn't keep his thoughts from wandering sometimes. He worried about the dogs. They foraged
far out across the tundra, but grew ever thinner.
And there was nothing to feed them. Two of the
old dogs had died; so had one of the puppies born
in the spring. The wolves didn't sing any more
across the tundra. Nukruk Agorek wondered if
they had left the home range to search for food.
He hoped that was the reason he didn't hear
them. He hadn't seen Agorek since the wolf had
rescued Little Mouse.

Slowly they lived from one hungry sleep to the
next, and still the long hungry night of winter
stretched before them. Always the search for food
went on, upshore and down. On sea and on land.
Everybody smiled, as always, because that was
their way. But worry can show through smiles as
well as through frowns. Ancient Grandmother
and Old Uncle rarely left their igloos. They were
too weak to walk very far. Little Mouse and
Keegor were getting better, but very slowly.

Areega Angun, especially, was deeply troubled. Finally he sent Nukruk Agorek to call the
men to his igloo. They came in from the ice igloos
and the hunting bidarkas, leaving only a few of
the youngest to man the fish lines and keep watch

for seal. As they crowded in, Nukruk Agorek followed and found himself a small corner beside the entrance way. No one had told him he might be present at the council. On the other hand, no one had forbidden him. Little Mouse, Natooka, and Ancient Grandmother were with P'tik Tok and Kiri in Oonatchek's igloo.

When they were assembled and seated—all the wily hunters, all the skilled fishermen who in other times provided well for the village—Areega Angun stood up and spoke. He was, he told them, deeply troubled.

"You have called me The-Wise-One. You have trusted me to lead you in the hunting and fishing by which we live." He paused and sighed sadly.

"It is time for me to turn to you. I have listened long and earnestly to my Little Man. But I hear no answer. And we starve. So I turn to you. What are we to do? What does the Little Man say to each of you?"

No one had an answer.

"Time and again we have gone downshore to the wide river mouth and beyond," Oonatchek said. "The fishing is no better there than here."

"We have followed the rocky beach upshore far beyond the end of the curve that rims the harbor to the north," Tagrak said. "We found neither fish nor sea animals."

"We have pushed out beyond the solid shore ice, where the stormy seas threaten from moment to moment to crush the bidarkas between the great ice floes," Imgok said. "But we bring in little. The fish have left these waters, and the seal and the walrus and the bear have followed them. Who can say how far they have gone?"

"Who can say?" Tagrak agreed. "Before the tern and the gull flew off, we sought to follow their sea flights. But we could never find where they flew to feed. And the beluga, too, have left the shore long since, and gone out into the deep open sea beyond our sight."

Areega Angun sighed.

"There is not a solitary caribou on the tundra. And little small game. The long night of winter is still not spent. And beyond the winter night, three, four times the moon will grow round and then shrink to the thinness of a curved lichen finger before we can hope to find ice-free rivers with salmon swimming upstream."

"It is too long to wait," Tagrak said. "We cannot survive until springtime unless we find food."

They were silent, each man thinking. Nukruk Agorek looked from one worried face to the next in the light of the sputtering oil wick. Then

Areega Angun spoke again.

"There is one here who has weathered many winters. I think he foresaw that this one might be bad. It may be he can help us now. It may be he can tell us what we must do. But he is too weak to leave his igloo."

He sent Nukruk Agorek to ask Old Uncle if a few of the men might confer with him.

"Help me up, Nukruk Agorek," the old man said, "and let me lean on your shoulder." The boy had an idea the old man was really glad to be consulted, even though being at the council took a great deal of effort.

Old Uncle listened while the men reviewed what had already been said. Areega Angun said he believed Old Uncle had foreseen the hungry winter.

"Who can say?" The old man shrugged. "Sometimes the waters teem with fish, and walrus and bear play on every rock. Then they leave, and the seas and the rocks are empty. Who can say why, or where they have gone?"

"We can only see what is before our eyes," Tagrak said simply.

"It is true, I feared the winter might be bad," the old man went on. "There were so many signs. So few of the spiderlike crabs that usually cluster on the seabed. So few small fish upon which the larger ones feed. And the beluga! So many beluga to feed on so few fish. Little left for the bear and the walrus and the seal. Nothing for us.

"When the boys crossed the tundra with me to the summer village, we saw no animals larger than lemming. The lichen is not plentiful enough to have kept stray caribou from the autumn migration. The tundra offers nothing."

"What does your Little Man tell you we must do?" Areega Angun questioned.

"Alas, I can tell you nothing." The old man shook his head sadly. "I would have told you if I had known. You are already doing all that can be done."

They were all silent then, sad and dejected, each man dreading the hardships ahead for those dearest to him.

"Well, then," Areega Angun said at last, "there is no time to waste. We must be about our work. We must fish without pause at the fishing holes and from the bidarkas. We must bring in what little the sea offers. Some of us may survive the winter. Spring may come early."

"One thing more the Little Man tells me." Old Uncle held up his hand as the men rose to leave the council. "There is one whose wisdom and experience have been gathered over more years than my own. Ask Ancient Grandmother to help you."

"A woman has never been known to attend the council, let alone address it," someone murmured.

"We will seek help wherever we can find it," Tagrak said quickly. He went with Areega Angun to bring her back to the igloo.

They settled the old woman comfortably on the fur pelts, and she listened to all they had to tell her.

"I marvel all the fish and the sea beasts can have gone so far from these waters," she said. "It would seem you have done everything that you can possibly do."

The disappointed men sighed and rose to leave.

"We thank you for listening, Ancient Lady," Tagrak said. "Now we must get back to the fishing."

"Not yet." Ancient Grandmother stopped them. "Give me a little time to think, to listen. The Little Man does not always speak at once."

The men sat down again and talked among themselves. After a while Ancient Grandmother was ready.

"Help me up, Oonatchek," she said. "I will address the council."

"It is not necessary that you stand," Areega Angun assured her.

"It would not be seemly to address the council without standing," she insisted, and rose to her feet. She was so frail and thin, she swayed a little when she stood. Areega Angun and Oonatchek stayed close to support her. But she waved them back and stood very straight and as tall as she, could.

"I have seen a harbor," she said slowly. She raised her head, and her faded old eyes seemed to be looking far away. The men listened intently. Her voice was low, but she spoke very clearly.

"I have seen a harbor," she repeated. "Very long ago. My Little Man helps me remember. We found many fish there, when there were none anywhere else."

The men questioned her eagerly.

"Where is this harbor?" Imgok asked. "Is it far downshore from the big river mouth? How many sleeps?"

"It cannot be upshore," Tagrak said. "We have gone to the outer end of the curved ridge of rocks that rims the sea above the village—and beyond. Farther than we have ever gone before."

"Oh, it is much farther," she told them. "Many,

many sleeps beyond the upshore rocks."

For a moment hope had lighted the eyes of each man, but now the light died in despair.

"So far?" Areega Angun shook his head. "Then it can do us no good. Neither the men nor the dogs have the strength to go so far. And there is not enough time left. Those waiting in the village would be starved before food could be brought back."

"There will be time," Ancient Grandmother insisted. "There is a way. I speak of a hidden harbor, opening on a different sea."

Journey to the Hidden Harbor

"A DIFFERENT sea?" Tagrak considered this slowly.

"How can such a thing be?" Imgok asked. "The sea is the sea. Always the same. It is there, below the igloos. How would we find a different sea?"

"Leave the shore," Ancient Grandmother told him. "Leave the shore and go across the tundra."

"To the summer village?" Oonatchek asked. "There is no sea there. Only the river."

"No, no. Do not go toward the summer village. Go upshore." Ancient Grandmother raised her arm and pointed. "But follow the sea only as far as the rocky beach that curves out above the village. Then do not follow the shore. Go straight ahead. Go on across the land."

The men crowded around her, hopeful again, interrupting each other with eager questions. "How far?" "How many sleeps?" "Is it open tundra all the way?"

"But, Ancient Grandmother." Nukruk Agorek was finally able to sandwich in his question. "How can we find the sea if we go inland?"

"I have told you, the harbor I speak of opens on another sea, beyond the mountains. Hills shelter the beach, and the harbor is deep and broad. You will find many fish there, I believe, and bear and walrus on the ice."

"My father used to tell of a very bad winter and of traveling a great distance for food," Areega Angun remembered.

"I, too, have heard such tales," Tagrak said, and turned to Old Uncle. "Have you heard of such a place?"

"I have heard the tales." Old Uncle nodded.

"And they are true. The place was very far away, but the people found much food. They brought back jade, too. Fine jade for hatchets and spear-heads. I never knew where the place was. I was still a child not long out from under my mother's parka. Ancient Grandmother herself was quite young, newly come to the village as my uncle's bride."

"It is at least a chance," Areega Angun said after a time of silence while the men considered the possibilities. "In how many sleeps might we reach this different sea?"

"Five sleeps, I should think," Ancient Grandmother told him.

"Is it open tundra all the way?" Tagrak asked.

"No, there is a river, and hills rising beyond."

"Tell us how we must go, Ancient Lady, and we will be on our way," Imgok said.

"Leave the sea where the shore curves out above the village, and go straight ahead—two long sleeps, I think; maybe a little longer—until you reach a broad frozen river."

"All open tundra to the river?" Oonatchek asked.

"I cannot tell you that," Ancient Grandmother said. "My Little Man does not show me."

"Mostly open tundra," Old Uncle told them. "I have been two sleeps and more above the village.

Only a few low hills. But I have never been so far as the river."

"Do we then go downstream to the river mouth?" Areega Angun questioned.

"No, no." She shook her head. "Turn again from the direction of the sea. Go upstream. The sleds will move easily over the smooth frozen river. In one long sleep the river should lead you through the first low ridge of hills and onto higher ground. Go on until high frozen falls block the river. Then turn aside. Across the high ground you will see higher crags and bluffs, hard to climb.

"Look for twin peaks, steep and high." Ancient Grandmother held up her hands and brought her fingertips together before her face. "Between them is open passageway, and hidden beyond lies the harbor and the sea."

Hurriedly the men made their plans. Half to go, half to stay behind with the women and the children, to bring in the meager daily haul of fish to keep the village from starvation.

They portioned out what little dried fish remained, those who were to stay behind urging more on those who were going, and the men who were going refusing all but their barest needs. Just enough to give men and dogs strength to push on.

Tagrak and Imgok drove two of the dog teams, and Areega Angun himself drove the third. He left Oonatchek to tend the fishing from the ice.

Nukruk Agorek wanted to go, and his father knew this. Areega Angun stopped a moment and considered it. Nukruk Agorek believed his father really wanted him to go along. But Areega Angun shook his head.

"You are needed here," he said. "Your Uncle Oonatchek will need all the help you can give him at the fishing holes until we return."

So Nukruk Agorek stayed behind. He worked hard with Oonatchek and the half-dozen other men left in the village, including the still-limping Keegor and weary Old Uncle.

Nukruk Agorek didn't mind working. What was hard was the waiting. The men seldom left the igloos over the fishing holes, each one sleeping a little while the others watched, letting no passing fish elude their bobbing lures.

For many sleeps they watched the crescent moon grow large and round as it circled overhead. When it slipped below the horizon beyond the sea, the water under the ice that floored the dark igloo still glowed, for with the fading of the moonlight, the stars shone brighter, and the northern lights flared like fire.

Whenever Nukruk Agorek carried fish up to

the village, he listened for his friend. But except for the wind, and the distant surge of the sea beyond the shore ice, the world around him was silent.

Two sleeps the teams ran across the crusted snow. Hope strengthened each man's endurance. They stopped just short of exhaustion for both men and dogs and set up snow-block igloos carefully, so they could use them again on the way home.

Before the third sleep they had traveled some distance up the frozen river. Before the fourth they had turned aside below the frozen falls and started toward the mountain range. Against the deep dullness of the black sky, the ragged crag tops shone in the light of the swelling crescent moon. Bare, windswept rock, snow patched in the hollows.

They halted the dog teams and looked up at the unbroken rock wall stretching before them, sloping back and very high right ahead, sloping jaggedly down a little to each side in the distance. They went on, choosing their way carefully across the smoothly drifted snow that hid the treacherous roughness of the tumbled boulders underneath.

Sudden clouds dimmed the moonlight, and

driving snow hid the ragged bluffs. They struggled on, men and dogs keeping close to each other, until they reached a fairly level place.

"Let us set up the igloo here," Areega Angun said, "and wait out the storm. At least the worst of it."

When the wind at last hurried the clouds across the sky, they again looked up at the cliffs facing them.

"I see no peaks," said Imgok.

"No passage through." Tuliak frowned.

"It may be the peaks are not so high, nor the passage so plain as Ancient Grandmother sees them through the eyes of her Little Man. Or with the eyes of her memory."

"Neither was the falls so high as Ancient Grandmother described it," Tagrak added.

They went in as close as they could to the high walls of rock rising before them. They searched far, walking toward the right, where the moon rises. But they saw no peaks, nor any passage through. So they turned back and searched far to the left, toward the horizon where the moon sets. But they found neither peaks nor passage, nor any foothold to climb the sheer bluffs.

The snow swept in again and forced them to turn. Feeling their way along the base of the cliffs, hungry, exhausted, disappointed almost to the point of hopelessness, they stumbled blindly back to the igloo.

The wind whistled across the mountains, bringing with it a smell of the sea. While some of the men unhitched the dog teams, Areega Angun stood still and listened to the screaming gusts.

Tagrak, about to crawl through the igloo entrance, straightened up.

"What do you hear?" he asked.

"Listen, and tell me," Areega Angun answered.

One after another, the men stopped and listened. Down the whistling wind, time and again, another sound came from across the cliffs. As the whistle of a wind gust died down, a rising note, high and clear, lingered faintly.

Torik herded the dogs into the igloo entrance and hushed them. The others waited, scarcely breathing. Then they all heard it, unmistakably: a triumphant, rising trill. The call of the-singing-ones!

"Wolves!" someone said.

"They sing from the other side of the cliffs," said another.

"The-singing-ones have long been gone from the hunting range behind the village," Imgok observed.

"This may be a strange pack. They may always have lived beyond the mountain barrier," Tagrak argued.

"That may be," Areega Angun agreed. "But if it is Agorek's pack—and it is true they no longer sing from the tundra near the village—if it is Agorek's pack, they have found the pass to the far side of the cliffs."

"Let us try calling them," Tuliak suggested.

The next time the wolf song came to them on the wind, Areega Angun sang out an answering call. But the wind was strong, and the cliffs were high. So his call was probably carried away, back toward the frozen river.

"When the wind dies down, Tagrak, you try," Areega Angun said. One after another they called, but there were no answers. Finally they crawled into the igloo to rest.

When they woke from that sleep, the wind had quieted. Again they heard the wolf songs from many places. Even far out across the tundra toward the horizon where the moon rose, it seemed, on the near side of the mountains. But nothing to lead them, and never an answer to their tries at calling.

"If Nukruk Agorek were here, he would know if Agorek were singing. He would know if these singing ones are Agorek's pack," Torik said.

"It is true I considered taking him," Areega Angun answered. "But I believed it was only my wish to have my son with me. Perhaps my Little Man was speaking to me, and I did not listen well. I think now that we must bring Nukruk Agorek here."

So Torik and Tuliak hitched the strongest dogs to one sled and started back to the village, a long journey of four sleeps.

The ones who stayed went on searching for the peaks and the pass leading to the sea. Most of their food was gone. What little had remained had been sent with Torik and Tuliak to sustain them on the journey back to the village. So half of the men foraged the tundra for food while the others continued the search. They managed to bring in enough rabbit and ptarmigan to keep them all alive, but barely. The dogs had to fend for themselves. They lived on the few lemming they found under the snow.

Torik and Tuliak were warmly welcomed back to the igloos. The women were glad to have news of their menfolk, although it could hardly be called good news.

Nukruk Agorek could scarcely believe his good

fortune when Tuliak said they had come to take him back with them. There was some talk of Torik staying behind, but Oonatchek said the few men left could easily bring in all the fish that came their way.

Tuliak and Torik questioned Ancient Grandmother about the twin peaks. She insisted they were there. She even took a stick and drew a picture in the snow. Two steep sloping cones, one a little smaller than the other, with a low v-shaped place between them.

"The highest point along the cliffs looks like that, a little," Torik said.

"But there is only one high point, and no passageway. At least none we've been able to find," Tuliak added.

"Go back and look again," Ancient Grandmother instructed them. "There are two peaks. And a pass between."

Nukruk Agorek loved skimming over the snow behind the dogs. He hoped the-singing-ones were Agorek's family; in his excitement he forgot he was hungry, forgot even to feel tired. He wanted to go on and on. But Tuliak and Torik watched the dogs and stopped when they needed rest.

Even before they reached the igloo at the base

of the mountain, they could hear the wolf song. But very faint and far away.

Later, with his father and the other men, Nukruk Agorek helped search along the base of the rugged cliffs, skirting the tumbled boulders, climbing up over them, searching down between them, always seeking that passage to the sea. And always, he listened.

Sometimes they heard nothing but the wind. Sometimes it seemed the wolf songs echoed all around them in the distance.

But never once was the boy able to recognize that special sound, that special tone, that was Agorek's.

Where Are the Twin Peaks?

THE MEN no longer looked for the peaks. There simply were no peaks. At least not twin peaks. The men sought only a way to the sea. And always, Nukruk Agorek listened for the wolf songs. He was so eager to hear Agorek's voice that he was reluctant to go back to the igloo when the tired men needed rest.

"Do you think this can be the right place, Father?" he asked Areega Angun again. "Ancient Grandmother says there are *two* peaks."

"The cliffs are irregular and rugged, you can see," Areega Angun answered. "She might mean any two rises, not necessarily that highest point before us."

"But there's only one that looks right," Nukruk Agorek protested. He touched his fingertips together in front of his face, as Ancient Grandmother had done.

"That's right," Torik agreed, making a steep peak with his touching fingertips, as Nukruk Agorek had done. "She even drew a picture in the snow."

So Torik and Tuilak drew the two cone shapes in the snow and pointed out the deep pass between them. The men considered the scratchings in the snow. Areega Angun shook his head.

"It is strange," he said. "We followed her directions, and they led us to this place."

"Yes, we followed as she told us," Tagrak agreed. "We crossed the tundra, went upriver to the falls, and turned."

"But——" Torik hesitated. "I didn't think the falls were very high. Did you, Father?"

"Ancient Grandmother said *high* falls." Nukkruk Agorek backed up Torik's opinion.

"High falls or low, one peak or two, what does it signify?" Imgok, always practical, cut short the discussion. "What we seek is passage to the sea."

"Oh, yes! Passage to the sea." One of the men lifted his head and drew in a deep breath. "I can smell the sea. It must be right there, just beyond the bluffs. But how do we reach it?"

Areega Angun sighed. "I had hoped the-singing-ones might lead us to the pass. But they do not answer our calls. I think the wind blows away our voices, and they do not hear us. I thought I was listening to my Little Man when I had Nukruk Agorek come from the village." He smiled sadly at his son. "But the-singing-ones still do not answer. We have not heard Agorek's call. It is likely these wolves we hear from across the mountain are a strange pack whose regular range lies there."

"The wind is quieter now than at any time since we have sought the pass," Tagrak said. "Let us try calling again. You try, Nukruk Agorek. Even though you haven't heard the song of Agorek, if he is among the pack he might hear you now, and answer."

So Nukruk Agorek called. Time and again he

called the sharp, rising trill of notes that said, "Come! Come!"

But there was no answer.

They went along the base of the cliffs, searching toward the horizon of the rising moon. They set up another igloo when they stopped to sleep. Again and again as they went on, Nukruk Agorek called. He called when the-singing-ones were silent; he tried to answer when the wolf songs came across the mountains on the wind. They couldn't know whether his calls carried across the cliffs or were only blown back behind him.

Another sleep went by. Still they found no passage between the rough rock walls slanting steeply up to the ragged cliff tops and the single cone-shaped high point, now some way behind them.

One more time of searching, one more sleep, and the men agreed they would have to give it up and go home, empty-handed, defeated. They were growing weak from hunger. The empty tundra below the mountains offered as little to sustain them as the strangely empty sea they had left. They prepared to set up one more igloo and sleep before they turned back. The hunters brought in two rabbits and a ptarmigan. Enough to keep them from starvation.

For Nukruk Agorek the misery was threefold. Beside the hunger and the disappointment of failure, which he shared with the men, he felt grief for his friend. Since the last time he had heard Agorek near the village, he had comforted himself with the belief that the-singing-ones had gone off to a better hunting range. Now he was sure they must have starved.

The wind had died down. For the moment, it was almost calm. The-singing-ones across the mountains were silent. Nukruk Agorek thought he'd try one more time, although he knew it was really useless. The strange wolves beyond the cliffs never answered—it wouldn't make any difference if they did. They couldn't be of any help, there on the other side of the mountain. And Agorek was dead. He was sure of that now.

The boy raised his head, as he had seen his wolf friend do many times, and cried out his woe. With far-carrying sad notes, he poured out his despair and his loss and his grief. While the song billowed out on the clear night air, his father and the others silently cut snow blocks and set up the last igloo, the same deep dejection in each one's heart. They had ceased their searching. They had given up.

Silence followed the song. Nobody had anything to say. Then, after a long moment, they heard a thin, clear thread of sound, coming from very far away. Maybe from across the mountains, maybe not. But in either case from far away, up toward the source of the river.

Nukruk Agorek answered and ran toward the sound. The waning half-moon, halfway down from the zenith, cast his shadow out before him. The next call was unmistakably from across the cliffs. Or, more likely, from atop them.

The sleds had not been unpacked. The men hitched up the dogs and followed. It was a long way. The hunger-weakened men, eager but weary, plodded after Nukruk Agorek along the base of the tapering bluffs. To their right, some way below, the course of the river paralleled the line of the bluffs.

The boy was well ahead of the men when he saw his friend. The wolf was above him on the flat top of a rock bluff. Nukruk Agorek had come a long way from the high peak that towered above the first igloo. The sloping bluffs were much lower here, only two or three times a boy's height, and not quite so rugged.

Agorek skittered back and forth, but he couldn't seem to find a way down. Nukruk Agorek finally found a snow-packed irregularity in the rock wall,

hacked toeholds out of the hard snow, and so was
able to climb up to the frantic dancing wolf on
top of the bluff. As always, the meeting was joyous, a matter of licks, laughter, nudges, hugs,
throaty growls, croonings, and tumblings in the
snow.

"Oh Agorek!" The boy's eyes sparkled as he regarded the handsome animal. "I'm so glad you heard me! I was afraid I might never see you again! I was afraid———"

He couldn't say it. But Agorek hadn't starved. Agorek wasn't even thin, as he had been the last time Nukruk Agorek had seen him. Now he was lean and lithe, vigorous and full-furred. The pale brown of his winter coat glistened in the waning moonlight.

The men were still some distance away when one of the wolf pack called, and Agorek, with a gay swipe of his tongue across the boy's cheek and an enthusiastic bump that bounced him off his feet, bounded off.

Nukruk Agorek watched him running off in the moonlight, along the top of the bluffs, back in the direction from which he had come. Then he saw the wolf turn left and disappear down the far side of the rocks.

The far side. The sea side! Nukruk Agorek gulped in a quick surprised breath, and began to look around. To his left, snow and rocks blocked his view. But to the right he could look down across the snow-covered boulder-strewn land all the way to the river. Ahead, that lower land narrowed as the river curved in toward the

the cliffs. And there, as far ahead as where Agorek had disappeared, he saw the falls! And they were *high*, as Ancient Grandmother had said. Three times as high as the falls where the men had left the river. The water, frozen into long threads of solid ice as it fell, flashed like fire as the light of the moon, just above the horizon, touched it.

He turned to call to his father and the others coming near below him. Instead, his eyes popped, and his mouth fell open. There before him were the twin peaks. The second peak couldn't be seen from the lower falls, because it was directly behind the other one. Even when they had searched along the base of the first peak they couldn't see it, because it was smaller and a little lower, and the high bluffs from which the first peak rose cut off their view.

He scrambled down the steep wall, missed one of the toeholds he had hacked in the ice, and swung by his fingertips till he regained his footing. After that, he went down more carefully.

"There *are* twin peaks, just as Ancient Grandmother said! The second one is there, *behind* this one!" He pointed beyond the cliff. "The falls *are* high! They're 'way up there!" He pointed upriver. "And Agorek went down on the other side of the bluffs!"

The words tumbled out, and his listeners, men and dogs, were caught up in his excitement.

"Come on, come on!" Torik shouted. "Let's start up!"

"Wait!" Tagrak called him back. So Torik stepped down from the first toehold.

"We turned off too soon," Imgok said. "Now I understand. But the Ancient Lady did not mention more than one falls."

"We turned off too soon," Areega Angun agreed. "Let us go on to the high falls and turn from there, as Ancient Grandmother directed."

"That is better." Tagrak nodded. "Up the face of the bluff is too risky. Nukruk Agorek might have been hurt."

Tired as they were, the men from the starving village went on, Nukruk Agorek leading the way to the falls. Ahead, the long rock ledge, over which the falls dropped, blocked their way. But to the left, the cliffs where the wolf had come from tapered down to the level of the land below the falls, leaving a narrow path around the base of the mountain. Beyond, the way lay open for them to follow a gentle rise back toward the pass between the peaks. For a moment they had to stop and marvel. There before them were the twin peaks, similarly cone-shaped, similarly steep. One a little smaller, a little lower than the other.

Just as Ancient Grandmother had said.

They hurried up the low slope, dogs barking, men puffing and panting, their quick drawn breaths clouding and freezing in the deep cold. Torik was first to look beyond the peaks; Nukruk Agorek and the others were not far behind.

Two ranges of low mountains came together at the twin peaks. At their feet, in the angle between the ranges, sloping beaches edged a wide frozen bay. The northern lights shone on the glittering ice. All empty and cold. But while they paused, taking in the scene below them, they heard a seal bark. Imgok saw a walrus, and Torik spied another. Far out they saw a white bear lope across the ice floes.

"There *must* be fish below that ice," Torik said.

"The Ancient Lady spoke truly," Imgok agreed softly. "Here there must be food to feed us all."

"We had only to follow Ancient Grandmother's directions," Areega Angun said. "She has always listened well to her Little Man. And she told us well. But it is not always easy to listen well, even to what is well told."

Relief to the Starving Village

THE MEN hurried out to cut fishing holes in the ice, leaving Torik and Nukruk Agorek to build an igloo at the edge of the frozen harbor. The boys cut snow blocks and fitted them together. The igloo wall was about halfway up when Nukruk Agorek's jade ax, chopping through the crusted top snow, struck against something more solid. The sound was dull. He hadn't struck against rock. He brushed back the under snow and shouted to Torik.

"Look, Torik! Wood! Driftwood!"

Nukruk Agorek took off a mitten and felt the wood. It seemed to be dry. The deep cold must have sealed it dry before the snows fell.

The men were already coming in, a heap of fish in one of the sleds. Enough to satisfy everyone's hunger.

"Look! Wood!" the boys called. There seemed to be a great deal of it, washed up on the beach through many summers. Areega Angun made a little pyramid of bits and pieces, and Tagrak struck a spark to start the fire. Imgok found a willow thicket in a small ravine that creased the lower slope of the second peak. Probably a running creek in summertime. He cut several of the longest wands—none of them were as long as Nukruk Agorek's arm—and they roasted fish over the fire. While the fish cooked, Torik and Nukruk Agorek roofed in the igloo and spread fur pelts over the snow floor.

The dogs ate their fill for the first time that long winter and then curled up in the snow, too comfortable and satisfied to bother crowding into the shelter of the igloo entrance.

It was a fine feeling, Nukruk Agorek thought, having enough to eat. But he couldn't really enjoy it for thinking of the hungry ones at home. They all slept briefly before hurrying back to the ice, each one thinking of the hungry ones at home.

By next sleep two sleds were well filled. Mostly fish—larger ones than they had seen all winter. A few seal. Even a walrus had fallen to Imgok's harpoon. And some of the precious driftwood was lashed to each sled. Again they ate and slept.

Then Areega Angun, Tuliak, and Nukruk Agorek were on their way. Tagrak, Imgok, Torik, and the other two men, all skilled at bringing in fish and bringing down the sea creatures who live in and near the water, stayed. One sled and half a dozen dogs stayed with them.

Areega Angun set the pace. Going out, each day's progress had been an uncertain venture. Knowing the way back, each day's journey was accomplished more easily and in less time. Going out, men and dogs were weak from hunger. Now at least they not were hungry. Most of all they were driven by fear of what they might find when they reached home. Hunger had long been there, and starvation had been near when Torik and Tuliak had returned for Nukruk Agorek. Finding the fish-filled harbor had taken many sleeps since then.

They made the journey back in four short sleeps. Where the land curved out above the village, they left the tundra and strained forward, anxious for the first glimpse of home. The igloos on the dune top and out on the ice glittered under the stars and a high crescent moon. An entire moon cycle had gone by since the men had set out to find the hidden harbor.

But the village looked strangely empty. Nobody walking around at all. And strangely silent. Not even one dog barking.

Areega Angun groaned, and Tuliak drew in a sharp breath that was almost a cry. Nukruk Agorek's fear made him feel as though he had been hit in the stomach. They ran the last part of the way along the shore.

When the sleds pulled up in front of the igloos, the barking of the dog teams brought a few of the women out of the igloos, and the men came slowly up from the fishing holes. A few dogs came out from the igloo entrances, too weak and listless to run or bark. Nukruk Agorek ran to his mother.

"Is everybody all right?" Areega Angun asked her.

"Not all right." Natooka shook her head. "But alive." She smiled and nodded reassurance to Tuliak.

By this time more people were gathering round. They looked at the high-packed sleds as though they couldn't believe what they saw. The travelers were welcomed with smiles. There was no strength for real joy.

Areega Angun began unpacking the food and passing it out. Tuliak took the first pieces for his wife. Then Natooka and Kiri took some for Ancient Grandmother and Old Uncle and a few others who had not the strength to leave the igloos.

But nobody ate very much, or very eagerly. Almost, it seemed to Nukruk Agorek, as though they had eaten so little for so long they had grown out of the habit of eating and had to relearn the skill. Even the dogs sniffed and licked at the frozen fish, leaving it and going back to it, before getting down to gnawing it.

"Fire is needed," Areega Angun said. "Quickly! Let us set a fire. Cooked fish will be easier for them to eat."

Some of the precious wood was stacked in a pyramid, and Areega Angun struck a spark. He sent Nukruk Agorek to collect egg-sized rocks and Tuliak into the igloos to bring out the cooking bowls. He pierced thin pieces of fish with a needlelike awl, threaded them on willow wands, and stuck the wands down in the snow around the fire so that the fish hung over the heat.

Nukruk Agorek dropped the stones around the edge of the fire to heat. As the moisture dripped out of the frozen meat hanging above, it hissed and spluttered in the fire. It was very strange, the boy thought as he worked. Ordinarily, everybody worked together. Now the others just huddled around the fire and watched as he, Areega Angun, and Tuliak worked.

"Here, Oonatchek, hold this fish over the fire," Areega Angun finally said, and handed his brother a small fish piece on a willow wand. He fixed fish on several more sticks and handed them out.

"Put snow in the bowls, my son," he directed, "and drop in bits of fish." Nukruk Agorek used his jade ax to chip frozen fish into each bowl. As the stones heated, he held the bowls close to the fire, one at a time, and Tuliak lifted the hot stones from the fire into the bowls. Tuliak wasn't very skilled at holding them between a pair of willow wands, and there was some splashing and spilling. But that didn't matter. It was important that they get hot food, a little at least, into these so nearly starved people. The broth wasn't as good as Ancient Grandmother's, but it would have to serve.

After the women had taken a little of the broth, several of them began helping the boys make more, mashing down the fish bits with a stick or a stone as it cooled. The others carried bowls of the warming, strengthening broth to Ancient Grandmother and Old Uncle and Tuliak's wife and baby son.

By the time everybody had had some of the comforting liquid, the roasting fish was cooked, and the reviving villagers were ready to enjoy it. At least able to eat it. Nobody ate very much; they knew that wouldn't be wise. Everybody could help a little when Areega Angun and the boys stored the food. Then they were all ready to crawl past the dogs in the entrance tunnels and sleep.

"It's so dark in the igloo," Nukruk Agorek said.

"Where is the lamp?" Areega Angun asked.

"We drank the last of the oil," Natooka said. "We needed it for food more than for light."

Nukruk Agorek ran from the igloo, brought back an ember from the fire, and blew it into flame. While he held it up, Areega Angun knelt down beside Ancient Grandmother and Little Mouse.

"You were gone many sleeps," the old woman said. "Hunger we have known. Starvation came very near. Another sleep might have been too late for some of us. Did I not counsel you truly?"

"You did indeed speak truly," Areega Angun told her gently. "The error was in our listening."

Little Mouse opened his eyes. "He is so weak," Natooka said in a worried voice. The boy seemed dull and drowsy, but he had drunk a little of the broth. And Areega Angun coaxed him to eat a bit of roasted fish before they all slept.

Areega Angun was anxious to be on the way again, but it was two sleeps before the sleds set out for the harbor beyond the tundra and the mountains. A fierce fast storm blew in and passed before all the men were strong enough to face the long trek across the open tundra.

Before the second sleep they gathered in Areega Angun's igloo. The story of the search for the hidden harbor, and how the-singing-one had led them to it, had been told and retold. Ancient Grandmother was thanked and praised for her wisdom.

The men considered the advisability of moving the whole village across the pass between the twin peaks. But the journey would be hardest on those least able to endure further hardship. And once there, there could be only snow-block igloos. The wood-framed, sod-block igloos were better shelter from the bitter winter weather. Fall was the best time to build the sod-block igloo. It was impossible now, before late spring had thawed the tundra turf. No, better to bring food to the village, rather than to move the village.

So the men conferred and reasoned together. No point in spending fruitless hours trying to bring in fish from a sea where there were none. Better most of the men of the village travel back and forth to the far harbor until they had brought back enough food to take the village safely through to the spring.

"Ten sleeps," Areega Angun said, twice opening his hand five fingers wide. "Ten sleeps to the harbor and back. Maybe less. For those who remain here, food enough to last at least ten sleeps. Maybe a few more.

"Three men to a team," he went on. "As soon as one team returns, a fresh team must set out. And at least three men must always stay here at the village with Old Uncle and the women and children."

After sleeping, they packed three sleds with furs for warmth in the igloos at the harbor, and lashed on an umiak and two bidarkas, so the men might hunt far out from the shore where ice floes floated on the waves and where larger fish as well as walrus, bear, and whale were to be found.

The dogs barked and strained at the leads, impatient to be off. The storm had cleared, and a swelling curve of the moon, aided by the stars and the northern lights, shone down on the new snow. Those who stayed behind watched from the igloos as the company, Areega Angun leading, moved up the shore.

Nukruk Agorek couldn't hide his disappointment at not going. Old Uncle saw that. And Keegor would have hopped all the way on one foot for a chance to go.

"You are young to be so honored," Old Uncle told the boys. "Tuliak is left with me to watch over the village while the others are gone. And we must rely on you for help. You," he addressed Nukruk Agorek, "and you, Keegor, although your injury still hinders you. It is a great responsibility."

"Anyhow, we won't be hungry," Keegor said. Nukruk Agorek nodded, trying to find some consolation in Old Uncle's words.

"Until now, we've been hungry all winter," Keegor said. "Hungry all winter, ever since the night began."

"I wonder why the Little Man didn't tell Ancient Grandmother about the harbor sooner." Nukruk Agorek looked puzzled. "We needn't have been hungry at all. We needn't have worked the empty fishing holes here at all."

"The-singing-ones knew sooner than we did," Keegor remembered.

"Don't expect the Little Man to do your work for you!" Old Uncle spoke sharply. "Every man must do his own work. Every man must provide shelter for his family and bring home food and furs to sustain and clothe them."

"But there was nothing here to catch," Keegor protested. "The sea was empty."

"Better we kept looking and went hungry," Old Uncle assured him "than that the Little Man should speak too soon. If the Little Man did it all, we'd get lazy. Everybody would get lazy. Nobody would bother to learn to lure the fish and to stalk the game. We'd forget how to make harpoons, how to set up igloos. The women would forget how to sew, how to fashion the mukluk that never lets in water.

"Bye and bye, everybody would sleep. All the

time, sleep. Bye and bye, everybody would die. Oh, no." Old Uncle shook his head solemnly. "Little Man is too smart. Never talks. Never talks until somebody's ready to listen."

Far away upshore the sleds were only a little moving blob of shadow on the starlit snow. Everyone who stayed behind knew how long, how exhausting, how dangerous the journey might be. Above the igloos the northern lights were fading, and the sky looked dull.

"But we always try——" P'tik Tok started to speak and stopped in midsentence. Nukruk Agorek saw a sparkle of reflected light in her eyes.

"Oh, look!" she said. The villagers looked where she pointed, and they all saw it together.

Far downshore the horizon was cut by a thin sliver of brightness. In a moment it was gone. It was the first brief break in the long night of winter. They still faced storm and hardship. But perhaps no more hunger. Springtime was still very far away. But the brief appearance of the sun's rim held promise of light and warmth again, and of another summer's plenty.

Elizabeth C. Foster lists literature, poetry, art and nature as her interests, and has always had a great fondness and sympathy for animals. Following graduation from Hyde Park High School in Chicago, she worked in the evening and after theater hours for Ashton Stevens, drama critic and columnist for the Hearst papers. Her first book, to which this is a sequel, was *Friend of the Singing One*. It was also written with Mr. Williams. Mrs. Foster now makes her home in Florida.

Slim Williams has had an ideal background for writing a story about Alaska. In 1900, at the age of 18, he went to what was then the territory of Alaska, where he lived for thirty-two years. He came out driving a dog team from Alaska to Washington, D. C., to get a highway to Alaska. His interests include trading with Indians and Eskimos, and catching wolves to cross with his huskies. Like the wolf in this book and his earlier book, all the wolves Mr. Williams caught proved trustworthy and harmless.